AFTERLIFE

AFTERLIFE

MAGIC & MECHANICALS BOOK 6

JESSICA MARTING

SHADOW PRESS

AUTHOR'S NOTE

While most of the books in Magic & Mechanicals can be read as standalones, *Afterlife* is a direct sequel to *Spellbound*. Major spoilers for that novel abound in this one. Reading *Spellbound* first is recommended.

CHAPTER 1

10 March 1890

Ezra,

It is long past the time you should have paid me a visit in London. The weather isn't ideal, but when is it, anyway? I have a new exhibition that opens in two weeks and I insist you attend. I can't imagine there is much to behold in the Liverpool art scene.

Of course, my home is open to you, as it always is. Bring a friend, if you want.

Julian Smythe

Ezra Thaddeus stood outside his ground floor flat's front door, bracing himself. His gloved hand clutched a brass key, but he couldn't bring himself to fit inside the lock just yet. On a whim, he pressed his ear to the door and strained to hear something of the inevitable chaos his new housemate was bound to be causing.

His only reply was silence.

He sighed. Quiet chaos was the worst. At least the door was cold, which meant the flat wasn't on fire. Again. He unlocked the door and cautiously stepped inside. "Claudia?"

A crash sounded in the kitchen. There weren't any accompanying screams, flames, or flooding water, which Ezra cautiously took as a good sign. He put away his coat in the foyer closet, and market bag forgotten on the tile floor, he strode to the kitchen to see what she had got up to this time. "What was that? You haven't tried to cook again, have you?" He found Claudia on her hands and knees in the kitchen, covered in white. He blinked, as if he couldn't believe his eyes.

She looked like an illustration in a children's book of a snow queen, albeit one who was melting in the sun. White dusted her shirt and trousers, was smeared in her long dark hair. When her guilty eyes looked up at him, he saw it streaked across her face. Not snow. Flour, presumably from the giant copper container of it his housekeeper set up on the counter. A container that had recently been refilled and now lay on its side, spilling its contents everywhere in puffs of white. "Sorry," said Claudia. "It just happened now."

"And you were scooping it up with your hands?" Relief flooded him at the knowledge that it was merely a mess he came home to.

"I ... well, not to put it back in the box." He and Claudia had had a few conversations about food and what to do with it after it fell on the floor.

"Why not use the broom to sweep it up?"

She stood and dusted flour off her loose brown trousers. "Where is it?"

Of course, Claudia wouldn't know where the broom was; she and Ezra seldom did their own housework. He'd spent their first few weeks of living together keeping her from trying to walk through walls and experimenting with matches. He opened a closet door inset into the wall, revealing a trove of cleaning supplies. He removed a broom and dustpan.

Before he could sweep up the mess, Claudia took them from him and did it herself, depositing the flour in the rubbish bin.

"What happened?" Ezra asked when she put them away. She reached for the carpet sweeper and pulled it out, fascinated.

He quickly rushed to her side and put it away, then closed the door.

"Mrs. Green uses that to clean the rugs," she remarked, sidestepping his question about the flour. "How does it work?"

"Suction and steam. Claudia, what were you doing with the flour?"

"Oh, that." She picked up the flour can and returned it to the counter. "It was an accident."

"Sober adults don't usually go about dropping it on the floor for fun, so I assumed it was." He squinted at her, searching for signs of intoxication. "You didn't get into my whiskey again, did you?"

She gave him her best withering look. "I did not. I was looking to see where you hid the biscuits and it fell over. You startled me when you came home."

"I didn't hide the biscuits this time. We ate the rest of them last night." Ezra hadn't been one for sweets until Claudia moved in. "I don't hide biscuits in baking supplies. I brought home a box of chocolates, anyway."

Claudia had already breezed past him before he could finish his sentence, leaving a trail of flour in her path.

Ezra sighed and followed her. He'd have to haul out the carpet sweeper himself before his housekeeper's next visit.

She'd already dug out the red velvet-covered box of chocolate truffles from his dropped shopping bag by the time he found her in the foyer. "Are you certain you don't want supper first? I can warm something for us."

She paused and considered his words. "I suppose so."

"Go get changed into clean clothes, and I'll get dinner on the table."

He hung up his coat and, with the box under his arm, returned to the kitchen. He warmed soup on the stove and slice off some bread from a loaf Mrs. Green baked during her last visit.

Claudia returned to the kitchen wearing a nightgown and one of his jumpers. "How was the market?" she asked brightly, helping herself to a piece of bread. She carefully buttered it.

Ezra kept an eye on the stove hob's tiny blue flame, waiting for the chicken soup to heat through. "There wasn't much we needed." Only sweets, which he'd been keeping in the house since she moved in. "Actually, I left to send a telegram." He braced himself to deliver his news. "One of my old university friends has invited me for a visit. His first major art exhibition will be opening at the end of the month."

Claudia paused and set down her bread slice. "You're going to Londinium?"

Ezra nodded, not bothering to correct her. "Yes."

"What will happen to me?"

"If Ivy and Merritt were in town, I would suggest you stay with them." His widowed stepmother and her new husband were currently enjoying an extended holiday in Spain. They didn't have any immediate plans to return to England.

"But they aren't in town." Claudia looked at him expectantly.

If they were, Ezra would have been reluctant to leave her with them, anyway. Chaos aside, he enjoyed her company more than he'd ever expected to. "They aren't. I thought you might want to go with me." He held his breath, waiting for her response.

It was immediate. Her face lit up in excitement, color appearing on her cheeks. "Really?"

The sight of her happiness always made his heart do a stupid little flip-flop against his ribs. "Yes."

"I haven't been to Londinium in years!"

Years was putting it mildly. As Ezra checked the soup's progress, he wondered if there was a word for reverse exaggeration. Perhaps there was one in Latin that Claudia was familiar with. "I thought you would enjoy a trip away. I'll book train tickets tomorrow."

"The train!" Claudia's dark eyes widened.

Ezra couldn't keep himself from smiling. It was one thing, of which there were many, that she hadn't yet experienced, something new she would share with him. He felt selfish at his wanting to be there with her as she learned how to be alive again, but was unwilling to step away. He never would have chosen one Claudia Drusilla Lucius, a resurrected Roman woman, to be his housemate, but here she was, and he'd found himself happier for it.

"I thought we could take the train to London and a dirigible to come home. That way you can try land and air travel."

"When do we leave?"

"We'll leave on Thursday," Ezra replied. "Two days from now. That will give us enough time to get you some new traveling clothes."

She nodded. "I suppose I'll need something appropriate for an art exhibit. Do you think my stola would be all right?" Before he could reply, she added, "I'm not being serious. I promise I will look like a lady and I won't embarrass you."

"You're not an embarrassment."

"What about that time at the market?"

Ezra nearly asked her which one she was thinking of, but stopped himself in time. "It wasn't an issue. You didn't know any better." There. That answer would suffice for the first time she accompanied him there and she helped herself to an apple off a vendor's stall. Or the time she tried to walk away with a knitted scarf without paying for it first because it was pretty. Or the incident where she climbed into a pen to play with a litter of sheepdog puppies.

"Well, I'll be on my best behavior, I promise."

Ezra ladled soup into a pair of bowls and joined her at the table. "We'll go to the shops tomorrow and get you something new for the exhibit," Ezra promised.

"Evening wear? Ivy's evening dresses are so beautiful."

His stepmother had embraced her clotheshorse ways since her mourning period had ended. "I don't see why not."

Delight suffused her features, and with it, a corresponding warmth spread through him. He hoped she would never lose that sense of wonder.

ONCE CLAUDIA HAD REMEMBERED how to walk, then learned how to walk in the current, often-ridiculous fashions, she had taken to strolling Liverpool in the mornings, content to ruminate in her thoughts. She had spent the first few days of being alive again having to remind herself how to breathe, how to recognize when she was tired or hungry, ordinary human functions that she hadn't thought twice about before she died over a millennium ago. She and Ezra had been pleased with her progress, with Ezra ceding to her desire to leave his flat unaccompanied after a few weeks. She understood some of his fear about her wandering alone. She supposed he respected her independence more than Merritt Sloan would, although his nervousness about it stemmed from concern. They'd been friends for years, since she haunted his flat.

Haunted.

Claudia didn't like that word. She didn't like to think of herself as haunting Merritt's flat when she was still dead. She just preferred staying on the mortal plane with living people. It had taken over a thousand years, but her refusal to leave worked in her favor, in a way.

Claudia strode with purpose along the sidewalks, taking care to avoid the steam-powered cabs and horse-drawn carriages that raced through the streets. The first time she had left the flat with Ezra, she nearly found herself flattened beneath the wheels of one. She couldn't recall the last time she'd seen Ezra so distraught. Crossing the street, she recalled when. It was after that awful night last autumn during a botched séance, when they'd huddled together in the bottom of Merritt's ornithopter's flight basket. It was the night they met. The night she'd been resurrected, struggling to remember how to breathe, how to move in her mortal body that hadn't felt so clumsy the last time she'd occupied it. The night Ezra had a chance to say goodbye to his late father.

Her route was familiar, one she took a couple of times per week. She supposed it would be faster to hail a steam cab, but she still found money and budgeting a little perplexing in this weird new century. She liked the walk, besides. Now that she could remember how to do it, it had become a pleasure to do so.

A light drizzle started to fall when she found herself at the front of Merritt's old flat, staring at the door. Taking care on the outside steps, she rang the bell for the house's landlady, Mrs. Malton.

The elderly woman opened the door with a smile. "Claudia! What a sight! I've just brewed some tea. Come in!"

Claudia smiled and followed her into the house.

Mrs. Malton lived on the first floor, the largest flat in the house. When she was a ghost, Claudia had enjoyed hanging about the landlady's home. The widow still had an active social life, unlike the house's other residents. Claudia had been happy to sit in with her and her friends as they chatted about their grandchildren and crafted together. The flat was filled with pillows embroidered by Mrs. Malton, the walls lined with paintings of birds and flowers. It was homey, the only such spot in the house. Mrs. Malton was also convinced that the house was haunted, although it wasn't as though Claudia could tell her that it had once been.

Even if she didn't like the word. There hadn't been any other spirits in the house as long as Claudia was in residence.

Mrs. Malton cleared away an overflowing bag of yarn from a worn blue velvet-covered chair. "Sit," she commanded. "I have scones. Do you want a scone? They're just out of the oven."

Claudia didn't care for scones—too dry for her taste—but she nodded to be polite. "Please."

"Butter?"

She smiled. "Why not?"

Mrs. Malton retrieved a tray from the kitchen bearing a copper tea set and a pair of buttered scones on plates. "I haven't seen you in days. What have I missed?"

"I'm taking a trip to Londi—London." She caught herself in time.

"I hope you have a pleasant visit, although I have to tell you that I despise London. Are you going with Mr. Sloan?" Mrs. Malton eyed her over the rim of her teacup, mischief in her gray eyes. Merritt had introduced them when he moved out of his upstairs flat. The landlady had been convinced that they were lovers since then, despite Merritt now being married to someone else.

"No. I think Mrs. Sloan would disapprove of such a visit. I'm going with my friend, the one you met when Merritt moved." She stumbled over the last word, unsure of her relationship to Ezra. Housemate, certainly. Tenant? She paid no rent. Ezra wouldn't hear of it even if she'd had the means to do so. What they shared transcended mere friendship.

Irritation crossed Mrs. Malton's features. "The haughty one with the superiority complex?"

"He isn't haughty." At least, Claudia hoped he wasn't. She wasn't sure what the word meant. She made a mental note to ask Ezra.

Mrs. Malton made a "hmph" sound but dropped the subject. "What waits for you in London?"

She thought about her family's estate close to the river's shore. Her pets, a pair of cats named Fera and Cyrus. And unexpectedly Marcus, who she hadn't thought about in years. She never thought it would be so easy to forget her reason for dying. Everything in her past life, reduced to dust and rebuilt a thousand times over.

Mrs. Malton was waiting for an answer. "An art exhibition. One of Ezra's friends is being celebrated for his work or some such thing," she finally replied.

"There are few things more intolerable than a man who thinks he's an artist, and that's an upper class man who thinks he's an artist." She gave Claudia a knowing look before delicately sipping her tea.

Not for the first time, Claudia wondered what the late Mr. Malton had been like and how he'd treated his wife. "Ezra studied art, too, and they're friends, so I suppose he has to be all right."

"I'm certain you'll fit right in with the artist crowd. You already dress like one."

She looked down at her plain dark trousers. She'd picked them out in a shop shortly after she was resurrected, paid for by Ezra. According to him, her taste in fashion veered toward clothing worn by lady aviators: sensible trousers, close-fitted jackets, short scarves. Claudia liked them only because she found everything else available to women too complicated, as lovely as she found the clothing. "They're comfortable," she said, a bit of a lie. Her stola had been comfortable. The brown wool garment, the only remnant of her old life, was neatly folded away in her bedroom at Ezra's, relegated to wearing around the house. "Anyway, we're taking a train to London. I've never—" She caught herself before she could admit she'd never taken one before. "I haven't been on a train in a very long time." Excitement thrummed through her at the notion.

"It's better than flying, I suppose." Mrs. Malton shuddered.

Claudia sipped her tea, then took a bite of scone. Even buttered, it was still dry, almost stale. She tried not to cough.

"Have you given any thought to what I said on your last visit?" Mrs. Malton asked after a pause.

Claudia immediately knew what she was talking about. "Sort of."

"I think you and Hugh would get on very well. You know I'd love to introduce you two someday."

Since they met, Mrs. Malton had told Claudia a few stories about her nephew, a man who had spent some time abroad doing the gods knew what. He was unattached and could use a unique woman like Claudia in his life, according to her. Mrs. Malton had already written to him about her, sending letters to his rented flat in Leipzig. If she hadn't been betrayed by Marcus, she would have let herself be intrigued, be flattered by Mrs. Malton's match-making efforts and the possibility of traveling to another country. If she hadn't met Ezra … something squeezed in her chest. She wasn't sure how she felt about him. He'd become closer to her than anyone else ever had, including Merritt, who she had known longer than anyone, dead or alive. Her relationship with Ezra felt rare and fragile. She suspected it was untreaded territory for him. It certainly was for her.

"You're woolgathering again," Mrs. Malton said.

She did that a lot. It would take a long time before she would stop living so much in her head. "My apologies. I suppose I'd like to meet Hugh sometime."

The landlady beamed. "He's promised to return home for a visit in a few months' time. I'm certain I could arrange for us to have supper together."

An uneasy feeling took over her as Claudia finished her scone out of politeness. She enjoyed Mrs. Malton's company, now that she was corporeal again. As interested as she was in meeting other people, how the hell was she going to explain her past? How could she invent a whole new person? Regret sank in as she realized what she'd done in agreeing to meet Hugh.

At least Ezra knew what she was.

CHAPTER 2

ORDINARILY, Ezra would sigh at the prospect of a long train ride, pack a novel and some drawing paper to help pass the time, and wait for it to be over. He had a sketchbook and pencils in his bag, but that was where the commonalities between other trips and today's ended. He was looking forward to the journey for the first time since he took off for university in London. His good mood was entirely because of the woman standing beside him, resplendent in a blue traveling dress and gray coat. Her long midnight-dark hair was held off her face in a braid, a gray hat topped with pink-dyed feathers perched atop her head. On anyone else, Ezra would have thought it looked silly, but it suited Claudia, somehow. She had described it as "festive" when she spotted it in a shop window.

They waited now on the platform, the earth beneath them picking vibrations as the London-bound train came into view.

Claudia started in excitement, then impulsively grabbed Ezra's hand as it lumbered along the tracks.

He squeezed it back, damning the barriers their gloves

kept between them. The train's whistle sounded as it pulled into the station, smoke issuing from its chimney before it came to a complete stop. Ezra had purchased a pair of first-class tickets, a luxury that would allow them their own small compartment. The carriage door opened, revealing a liveried porter who nodded in their direction and checked the tickets in Ezra's free hand. "You'll be upstairs," he said crisply, before stepping off the train and picking up their luggage.

Claudia gave Ezra a delighted smile at the mention of a private upstairs compartment.

The porter picked up their bags as if they weighed nothing, carrying them up a winding staircase with an iron railing. Plush red carpet padded their footsteps, shockingly clean for public transport. The train's first level was decorated with the same red carpet, its walls covered with heavy copper-colored paper on which paintings of trains and dirigibles were affixed. To Ezra's trained eye, the artwork looked generic and soulless, but he supposed he should be pleased that the railways had made an effort at all.

The train's top level was divided into private compartments, each narrow door's window covered with a small red curtain. The porter opened one marked 5B in ornate brass figures, holding it open to leave their luggage on the floor. "Refreshments will be served after the train has left London, with a light meal available at five. We expect to be at King's Cross at half-seven," the porter reported.

Ezra knew this, having purchased the tickets, but instead of snapping at him for parroting back information a ticket-holder should already know, he nodded. The old Ezra would have done that, the one he'd been before the séance that changed his life. "Thank you." He slipped the man a shilling.

The porter nodded, giving him a knowing smile.

"Much appreciated, sir. Enjoy your journey." He closed the door behind him.

Claudia turned around, taking in the compartment.

It wasn't a sleeper train; this one only embarked on day trips, so the furniture was limited to a pair of mahogany chairs bolted to the floor, a polished wooden table, and a coat rack. Ezra took off his hat and draped it over one of its hooks, then his coat. "Claudia," he said.

She looked down. "Oh, yes." She unpinned her hat and unbuttoned her coat.

Ezra helped take it off her shoulders. The faint scent of her frankincense perfume reached him, the smell of the outdoors. Of antiquity, as well. Beneath it was something that was uniquely Claudia and he could never tire of it.

She crossed the short distance to open the window drape, letting in flat gray spring light. It haloed the wisps of hair that had come free from her braid. "Is this what all train travel is like?"

"No. You may be disappointed by the Underground."

"What's that?"

"Subterranean mass transit in London. One of the prides of the city, believe it or not."

"Better than a horse and cart, certainly." She turned around and closed the drape. A sconce on the wall dimly glowed. She touched the switch at the base experimentally, fascinated as its flame grew brighter. "Is this electric or gas?"

"Likely electric."

"Huh." She stared at it in amazement. "What a time to be alive again."

In all their months together, Claudia had never been forthright about what happened in her previous life, how she died, why she haunted a Liverpool flat for centuries. When Ezra thought about it, he wondered if she remembered at all. He could hardly remember his years in the schoolroom, and that was only little more than a decade ago.

"Will we have time to see the river?" she asked. She settled into a chair and arranged her skirts around her.

He hadn't expected that question. "You *want* to visit the Thames?"

She shrugged. "Why not? That's where my family's estate was."

He hadn't expected that tidbit of information about her old life. "What did your family do?" he asked carefully, not wanting to pry too much. What a lie. He wanted to know everything he could about her. It was odd for him, given that he scarcely cared about others' backstories, but theirs wouldn't have been as fascinating as that of a woman who originally lived over a thousand years ago.

"Farming, mostly. I lived with them longer than was usual until I had what you could call a broken engagement." A shadow fell over her usually cheerful expression.

What the hell? *Engagement?* Had she been married before she died? Before he could ask about that, the train's whistle sounded. Vibrations ground out beneath their feet and it lurched forward.

Claudia squealed in delight and grabbed the chair's armrests. She opened the drape again to peer out the window as it pulled away from the platform. Ezra took the seat opposite her, the table separating them.

"How fast does this go?" she asked.

Who was she engaged to, why did it end? "I'm not sure." Thirty miles an hour? Forty? How far away was London, exactly? He didn't have a clue. The part of his brain that should have processed numbers and formulas was defective, according to his late father. It was why he'd been drawn to art in the first place. Perspective was so much simpler to figure out than how long it would take to get to London from Liverpool aboard a luxury train.

The train picked up speed.

Claudia cautiously rose to her feet and looked out the window. Ezra didn't have to join her to know she was taking in a view of a dismal countryside on a gray spring day. "Tell me about your artist friend," she said, returning to her seat.

"Obviously, Julian is a more successful artist than I ever was, if he's been welcomed to a gallery."

"Your work is beautiful and I'm certain it could be featured in a gallery, too."

He tried not to preen under her praise.

"Does he paint oils like you do?"

"Among other mediums. Julian is a sculptor, primarily, at least he was when we were at university. I suppose you would know sculpture."

She looked at him quizzically, raising a dark eyebrow. "Why? Because I lived during the Roman occupation?"

"It was such a small community, considering."

"Life was *hard* in Londinium in the fourth century. I didn't have time to stroll about museums. And I don't think England was ever renowned for its marble supply."

She'd lived and died in the fourth century. That was the second personal thing she had revealed this afternoon. "Were you born there?" he asked.

"No, but I don't remember my life before. I think I was born in what's now Florence, but I'm not certain. My family traveled to Londinium when I was still a baby. I was perhaps two years old when we came to England." She shrugged. "I don't think my family was important enough to be remembered through the ages and we didn't keep records the way people do now. I'm not even sure how old I was when I..." She paused before she could talk about dying. "Before. Maybe twenty-two or twenty-four."

"No birthday parties, then."

She shook her head and changed the subject. "Anyway, you haven't told me about your friend's work. Sculpture, in the Roman style if you thought I might know something of it?"

"That was one of his fascinations when we were at university. I'm pleased to hear it's paid off for him." That was a bit of a lie. Jealousy rose in him when he thought of Julian's exhibition, the risks his friend had taken to get to that point, and the success he'd achieved. What had Ezra done since they'd left university? He sketched and painted sparingly, lived off his mother's inheritance. He'd kept up a steady stream of mistresses, and burned bridges with his father and stepmother. Guilt twinged through him when he thought of his father and Ivy, even though they had eventually reconciled. Not to mention, there hadn't been a mistress to speak of since Claudia crashed into his life.

"Julian was interested in ancient Roman and Greek art," Ezra continued. "He took a few trips to Italy and Greece when we were students. I went with him a couple of times."

"Have you been to Florence?" Claudia leaned forward in anticipation.

"Rome, actually."

"I don't think I've been." She sighed and looked out the window. "Is there anything I need to know about artist etiquette? I don't want to embarrass you or your friend while I'm there."

A light rain misted the glass in blurry streaks. "You don't embarrass me."

"I did at the market and that time I nearly burned down the flat. The neighbors were not amused."

"You hadn't used money in a few hundred years, so the market incident was forgivable." There had been multiple market and fire incidents, but Ezra didn't specify which one.

"My father handled our money, so I wasn't used to it."

"And by fire, do you mean the time you tried to smoke one of my cheroots or cook?" he asked.

"Either one."

Ezra had given up smoking due to her shenanigans with fire. It was just easier that way. The urge to do so was still with him, but he'd rather contend with the cravings than see his home burned down. "You're still learning to live in the modern era. A few mishaps with household appliances are to be expected. That fire was so small that it's hardly worth getting upset about."

She smiled, the sight of which would never not make his heart skip a beat. "You've been very patient with me. You don't know how much I appreciate that."

"I could say the same. I've told you things I've never said to another soul." He thought about their first meeting the previous autumn, how she had materialized in front of him, unable to walk, not knowing how to breathe. How they'd held each other on the floor of an ornithopter's flight basket, weeping over their shared terror. He'd never cried in front of anyone in his life until that night, including when his parents died.

She looked like she wanted to reply, but couldn't find the words. "There's a lot I haven't told you or Merritt. Not because I don't want to, but I don't know how."

Was she talking about her fiancé? If she was, why was he envious of a long-dead man, one who had apparently cast her away? "Why not?"

"Because none of it is relevant now. Maybe one day I'll find the words."

He tried to joke. "In English or Latin?"

"English, of course, unless you speak Latin and forgot to tell me."

"Not a word." Yet another shame of his.

"No bother, no one else speaks it, either."

"Doctors and solicitors do." At least, his father, the great Dr. Thaddeus of patent medicine fame, did.

"Well, when I'm ready to talk about it, I'll speak about it in English." She leaned back against the chair.

A crisp knock at the door interrupted Ezra before he could reply. He opened it to reveal a liveried porteress with a large brass cart next to her.

"Tea for either of you?" she asked. The black feathers on her regulation striped cap bobbed when she tilted her head, waiting for his answer.

"Please," Ezra replied.

The porteress poured hot water over leaves in a pair of heavy mugs. She set small boxes of milk powder and sugar cubes on the table between them. "Biscuits?" she asked.

Claudia nodded eagerly and the porter set a small paper box on the table. She had yet to meet a biscuit she didn't like since Ezra had known her. Or chocolate or tarts or cake.

Ezra gave her a coin, which she slipped into her apron. "Thank you, sir. I'll see you again in an hour." She left the compartment, closing the door behind her with a click.

Claudia opened the paper box and peered inside. "They have raisins."

"They're all yours." Ezra despised raisins.

"Thank you." She removed a tiny oatmeal raisin biscuit and bit into it, bliss written across her face.

Ezra swallowed a mouthful of tea and tried not to shudder at its bitter taste. Hardly the quality of beverage he would expect aboard this kind of train, but he wouldn't complain. He caught Claudia's eye, and she gave him a look that said she knew how he felt about it. Not for the first time, he wondered how two people could know one another so well, yet not at all.

What the hell happened to her a millennium and a half ago in Londinium?

CHAPTER 3

THE SUN WAS LONG GONE by the time the train lurched to a halt in London. Any stars overhead were obscured by light from the surrounding buildings and smoke that belched from trains and chimneys. When Ezra helped Claudia step off the train, she looked up to see a mess of mechanical aircraft zipping about overhead, from open-topped ornithopters to dirigibles. What struck her most was the smell. She didn't recall the Londinium of her old life stinking to high heaven like its current iteration did. She couldn't put a name to the smells, either, other than a mix of old food, body odor, and burning wood. The latter took a moment for her senses to fully register, and for a moment she thought she might be sick. The fire was so close she could taste it. She gasped and coughed, desperate to get fresh air into her lungs, before she realized she wasn't surrounded by it. It would not suffocate her again.

"Claudia?"

She coughed again before meeting Ezra's gaze. There was concern in his icy blue eyes, a shade not unlike the center of a flame. She closed hers for a moment, willing herself not to associate Ezra with fire and smoke. Her heart thudded so hard against her ribs that she thought he might hear it over the train platform's din. What had caused that reaction when she had been fine around fire before? Was it due to being back in London?

"Claudia," he repeated, more urgently this time.

"It's nothing. I'm all right," she said, pasting a smile to her face. Behind her, she was dimly aware of a porter hauling out their bags.

Ezra didn't look convinced. He took her hands in his, the feel of him solid and dependable.

She relaxed a little as her scattered, panicked thoughts reassembled themselves into something more normal. Ezra wasn't Marcus. He wouldn't let her die in a fire. For a moment, regret flared in her. Why had she been so eager to return to Londinium, again? To prove to herself that the original city was dead and buried a thousand times over? She shook it off and squeezed his hands, more to reassure him she was all right than herself. "I'm fine," she lied. "I wasn't expecting it to smell so terribly." She wrinkled her nose to illustrate her point.

Ezra took a deep breath and coughed. "Damned if you aren't correct on that count. It won't smell like this where we'll be staying, I promise."

She nodded. She hoped she didn't look as nauseated as she felt and that wherever they left in the dirigible back to Liverpool wouldn't have the same stench. Or where they stayed in London, for that matter.

They had walked only a few yards along the platform before a voice called out, "Thaddeus!"

Ezra stopped in his tracks.

Claudia followed suit, looking around the crowded platform but not seeing a familiar face. Not that she knew many people, and no one who lived in London. When she glanced at Ezra, she saw his face had split into a grin, so unlike him, and he held up his hand, the one that didn't have a hold on their luggage.

"Julian," he replied, as a man about his age bounded up to him. Ezra held out his hand to shake, but the other wrapped him in a hug instead.

Age was where the similarities ended. Where Ezra was fair-haired and blue-eyed, the other had dark hair worn unfashionably long and dark eyes. Ezra's clothes were carefully chosen and perfectly pressed; Julian's oversized gray wool coat was old and patched. Streaks of paint marred the frayed cuffs, his boots scuffed and trousers mended. His disheveled appearance aside, there was an air of confidence around him, like he was used to walking in a room and commanding the attention of everyone in it without trying.

"I wasn't expecting to see you at the train station," Ezra said.

"Bollocks. Of course, I wouldn't leave my friend to get to my house on his own. That's simply rude." Julian turned to Claudia. "Speaking of rude, you haven't introduced me to your wife. You didn't even tell me you *have* a wife, you bastard."

Something in Claudia twisted at the word "wife." She wasn't sure how she felt about that.

Ezra's nostrils flared and a shadow crossed over his features. Just as quickly, it was gone, replaced with a smile. "This is Claudia Lucius," he said. He omitted the rest of her name, as it wasn't fashionable to be Claudia Drusilla Lucius in the nineteenth century. "Claudia, meet my friend, Julian Smythe, artist."

"I suppose I'm an official artist now." Julian took Claudia's hand and kissed the back of it with more flourish than she thought necessary.

Was it her imagination, or did that shadowed look return to Ezra's face? "I'm not his wife," Claudia said, not wanting that charade to continue. "We're very close friends."

Ezra blinked, but didn't comment.

Julian's face lit up with a knowing smile. He clapped Ezra across the back. "I thought for a moment you'd given up your ways, but I see you haven't."

Ways? What ways? How did she fit into his ways? Curiosity pulled at Claudia, but she didn't pry.

Julian helped himself to Claudia's bag. "Follow me. My coach is waiting outside the station."

"We'll be staying at my house," Ezra said.

"How can you attend my house party if you're staying at your house?" Julian asked.

"I thought this was an art exhibition."

"It *is* an exhibition. It's also a party. This is the first time most of the people I've ever liked have been together at the same time since university, and it's worth it to celebrate. I have a room for you and everything." Julian gave Ezra a beseeching look, not unlike a small boy pleading with his father.

Nervousness wracked Claudia. As much as she liked people, she knew nothing of house party etiquette. She knew little of art exhibition etiquette, since she and Ezra inevitably veered off track whenever the subject came up. Between the train station platform's smell and the full days ahead, she started to regret this trip to London.

Ezra glanced at Claudia, then at Julian. "Could I have a word in private?"

Julian's dark eyes widened in surprise, but he nodded. "Of course." He turned away, Claudia's bag still in his hand, and took a few steps away from them.

Ezra leaned over. His breath tickled a wisp of hair by

her ear that had escaped her braid. "We can stay at my house if you wish," he whispered. "I won't make you stay anywhere you don't want to. I didn't know Julian would insist on a house party. I'd hoped he'd outgrown such events."

She forgot to answer. His nearness affected her in a way it hadn't before. "Oh?" was all she could muster.

"Say the word, and we'll stay at my house in Mayfair."

"No," she replied. "You decide. I know you won't leave me to the wolves."

He looked torn, undecided. "I should have expected this. God, I'm an idiot," he muttered.

"Why don't we stay a night or two with Julian for the sake of politeness, and then we'll stay at your house?" she suggested.

"I haven't prepared you for one of Julian's house parties," Ezra said slowly, mulling over her suggestion.

"How bad could they be?"

He blinked, as if remembering exactly who he was speaking to. "Well, you *did* live through the Roman era and all its debauchery."

That didn't bode well for Claudia, who, as a middle-class unmarried woman and her family's only daughter, hadn't attended over the top gala affairs the first time she was alive. Especially in such a hardscrabble place as Londinium, but she didn't want to spoil Ezra and Julian's fun, so she nodded instead. "Yes." She could at least pretend to have been a worldly woman in this new century. Perhaps Julian, an eccentric artist, would be charmed by it.

Trepidation didn't leave Ezra's expression, but he nodded. He raised his head away from her to call out, "Julian."

The other man turned around, all smiles. "What will it be?"

"How long is this party?"

He shrugged. "As long as people feel like visiting with me. At least three or five nights, I'd expect. This is a major debut according to *everyone*. The exhibit opens tomorrow."

"We'll stay a night or two," Ezra said.

"That's a start. I'm certain I could convince you to stay a little longer." He winked at Claudia. She didn't know how to feel about that. Julian inclined his head ahead of them. "Follow me. My driver is waiting."

JULIAN HADN'T CHANGED at all since the last time Ezra saw him, which had to be at least a couple of years. Ordinarily, Ezra would have been delighted to see a former classmate in the same arrested development he was in: no spouse, no children or other responsibilities aside from his art, not that Ezra devoted much time to the latter since his university days.

He caught Julian giving her an appreciative once-over and his feelings about their reunion shifted.

Ezra tried not to let it bother him, although he knew his old friend would ask about her at his earliest opportunity now that he knew they weren't married. Both of them had a predilection for women like her, petite brunettes with generous hourglass-shaped figures.

A gigantic steam carriage waited outside the train station, one of many, but Ezra knew this one had to be Julian's. It was oversized and ostentatious, its chimney reaching eight feet in the air. Steam lazily curled out of its spout. At the front was a covered driver's box, where a man in livery waited, heedless of the spring drizzle that misted around him. When he saw Julian, he started to get up, but Julian held his hand. "Don't worry about this. They haven't got much," he said. To Ezra, he said under his breath, "Bryson is a new hire. He thinks too highly of both our positions."

"I thought that was the point of a driver."

"My God, Thaddeus, I'm capable of carrying my own bags." He opened the carriage door and tossed Claudia's case inside without a care. "Well, bags, anyway."

Ezra set his own inside, then helped Claudia inside the vehicle. Before he could take the seat next to her, Julian scampered inside, leaving Ezra to sit across from them. That same appraising look crossed his face as Claudia arranged her skirts around her. It was a nervous habit of hers, he'd noticed.

The notion that he'd made a mistake in agreeing to come here crossed his mind, irrational as it was. Unexpected jealousy gnawed at him like a hungry dog with a bone, another bizarre emotion.

"How did you two meet?" Julian asked Claudia.

They'd gone over their cover story aboard the train over a light supper. "Claudia is a friend of my stepmother's husband," Ezra replied. It was technically the truth.

Julian's brows rose in surprise at the mention of Ivy. "The bitch moved on, did she? That was quick. It's been, what, two years since your father died?"

Ezra cringed, remembering how he used to disparage her before they reconciled. "Longer than that, and Ivy and I have made up," he replied stiffly. "We've actually become friends, believe it or not." Shame flowed through Ezra at the stricken look on Claudia's face. He'd been truly awful to Ivy when his father was still living, and for a great deal of time after he died.

Julian pinned Ezra with a stare. "You can't be serious. You two were mortal enemies!"

"We've signed a proverbial armistice." Ezra changed

the subject. "What kind of exhibition are we walking into?"

"This collection takes its inspiration from pleasure and hedonism." Julian again spoke to Claudia, sending a lascivious look her way.

Her eyes widened in understanding, her only reaction. Unless Ezra's imagination was running away from him, she actually shrank back against the seat half an inch.

"Food, drink, fucking, you know."

Ezra felt himself blanch.

Claudia coughed.

He didn't know why he felt this way. It wasn't as if Julian hadn't been using sex as a metaphor for everything for as long as they'd known one another. He'd been an idiot for thinking that perhaps his old friend had a gallery full of landscapes to show off.

Julian lifted a dark eyebrow at Ezra's reaction. "Are you surprised by this? How long have we known each other?"

"I suppose I shouldn't be."

"You would be surprised at the market for erotic art right now, Ezra, at least in London. I've also had interest from a gallery in Paris. In retrospect, I should have debuted there, but I couldn't help but rub my success in the faces of everyone who tried to talk me out of building clockwork-powered penises." He paused. "Penii? What's the plural form?"

Claudia let out a nervous giggle. "Do I want to ask why?"

"Of course, one should *always* ask why when it comes to art. You may not like the answer, if there is one, but it should be questioned."

"Do I really have to look at mechanical penises and praise you for your artistic vision?" Ezra asked.

"Is that the correct plural form?"

"How the hell should I know?"

The carriage lurched to the left, drawing a squeak from Claudia. "English is a stupid language," she said, glancing out the window. It wasn't the first time she had said as much in Ezra's presence.

Julian gave her an appreciative look. "I like her, Thaddeus."

Ezra already knew he did. Knew it, and hated it.

DESPITE HER EARLIER TREPIDATION AT the train station, Claudia's curiosity was piqued about everything that lay ahead. It was all she could do to keep herself from pressing her face against the carriage's windows to better see Londinium's sights. Where simple wooden houses once stood, there were now buildings taller than anything she'd seen in Liverpool. Gas lamps lined the streets, their flames glowing brightly as nighttime fell over the city, and cast everyone walking beneath them in beatific light. Steam vehicles and horse-drawn carriages alike crowded the road beside them.

Julian's house turned out to be the largest she had ever seen, a surprise considering his raggedy appearance. It was bigger than Ivy Thaddeus's home, which had been the largest she'd ever seen since her resurrection. Even before she died, Claudia hadn't seen homes on the same scale as Ivy's, let alone Julian's. It stretched four floors into the sky, dwarfing its comparatively modest neighbors. An ornithopter rested on the flat roof. The house glowed green and gold in the waning light, a bizarre beacon in the darkness.

As the carriage pulled into its front drive, she realized it was a reflection from the thousands of brass and copper-colored tiles affixed to the house's entire exterior. Definitely eccentric. Claudia wasn't sure if she liked the house's appearance. It reminded her of the collection of copper boxes used to hold sugar and spices in Ezra's kitchen. She half-expected to see it tip over and spill flour across the street.

"Your rooms are waiting," Julian said before alighting from the carriage. He reached for Claudia's hand to help her out.

When her feet touched the ground and she turned to face Ezra, he had an unreadable look on his face, another one.

"Unless you wanted one room? I wasn't certain if you're the kind of couple who sleep together," Julian said, glancing at each of them.

She hadn't thought about rooms at all. Drat it, she was terrible at being alive in the nineteenth century. Glancing at Ezra, she waited for his reaction.

"You did assume we were married," Ezra pointed out.

"There are different kinds of marriage arrangements."

"Are they the blue rooms?" he asked.

"Of course. I know how much you always liked them."

He shrugged. "The blue rooms will be fine for us."

Claudia refrained from asking what they were, sure she would find out soon enough.

The house's copper-paneled front door opened and a liveried servant hurried out to the drive. "Sir," he said to Julian, then collected the bags from the carriage.

"The other guests have already arrived," Julian said. He offered his arm to Claudia. Not wanting to be impolite, she accepted it. Ezra walked on her other side.

Julian gave her a wry smile. "Ezra, I think you'll know most of them, anyway. Claudia, I promise everyone inside is … well, not nice, exactly. Affable. Nice is too boring."

Another liveried servant held open the door for them.

From the foyer, she could hear the din of voices in conversation, punctuated by the occasional gale of laughter. She cast a nervous glance to Ezra, who gave her a reassuring smile in return. Claudia racked her brain and tried to remember the last time she'd been in the presence of so many people. When she was alive, it had to be at a party celebrating the birth of her cousin Flavia's son, his name lost to time. After she died … was it the Christmas feast Mrs. Malton hosted in her flat some five or six years ago? With about eight people in attendance, mostly her widowed friends? Here she was, about to make her second debut with a bunch of strangers. Her palms grew sweaty and she had to resist the impulse to wipe them against her skirt.

The servant took their coats. "Mr. Palfrey took the liberty of opening your last bottles of 1882 claret half an hour ago," he reported briskly.

"What a bastard," said Julian.

"Shall he be removed from the premises, sir?"

"Of course not. It's excellent claret and a joyous occasion. I'll haul him to the back garden and pretend to thrash the shit out of him on general principles after I've had a glass or two myself." He sighed melodramatically. To Claudia and Ezra, he said, "It seems we have some catching up to do with the other guests. Follow me."

Her nervousness aside, Claudia looked forward to meeting the other guests. In her old life, she'd never been one to shy away from a party. Still, she reached out for Ezra's arm, needing his support. He looked down at her, a reassuring smile on his lips.

The room he led them to was just as ostentatious as the exterior of the house. Its walls were painted a deep red, covered over in what looked like black lace. Electric sconces lined the walls, casting shadows over the faces of the other guests. She thought back to the party for Flavia's son, how bright and airy her cousin's house was. This room felt close despite the size, and unsettling.

"You've redecorated," Ezra commented.

Julian ignored that remark and addressed everyone else. "Look who finally deigned to visit us all the way from Liverpool!"

Every face in the room turned to look at Ezra and Claudia. Immediately, their expressions shifted to ones of delight at seeing an old friend. She wondered how long it had been since his last trip to London. They swarmed around him, offering hugs and handshakes, punctuated by the occasional, "Where the devil have you been hiding?"

Claudia instinctively moved closer to him as the air felt like it closed in on her. Ezra glanced at her in between greeting his friends. She must have given away something that betrayed her discomfort, because he quickly reached for her hand and squeezed it. Bolstered by the contact, she released a breath and pasted a smile to her face. Once upon a time, she had been a woman who loved parties, loved being around people. She wanted to be that person again. Like breathing and walking, she just had to remember how to be social.

"Wine?" A young man with close-cropped red hair held up a bottle. His face was flushed, nearly blotting out his freckles.

"Is that my 1882 claret?" Julian demanded.

"It is. The best I've ever had."

"Palfrey, you are a thieving bastard." Julian's tone was light despite the insult.

Palfrey shrugged. His half-unbuttoned shirt slid down his shoulder, revealing a patch of pale skin. "I'll have you know my parents were married six months before I was born." To Claudia, he said, "Can I get you some wine?"

"Not yet," Ezra replied. "We've had a long journey. I think we would prefer to see our rooms before we join in the revelry." He lifted a brow at Claudia.

It was as if he could read her mind, sense her discomfort. She nodded.

Unperturbed, Julian said, "Of course. You know your way around. Just come back soon."

Ezra led Claudia down a corridor off the red room. "Are you all right?" he asked, his breath ruffling her hair.

A shiver coursed through Claudia at the sensation. For half a second, she wondered what it would feel like if he pressed his lips to the sensitive spot under her ear. She'd forgotten until now how much she'd liked that the first time she was alive. "I'm fine. It's just been a very long time since I've been around others my age."

They reached a vestibule, its floor marble slabs. Staircases branched off on either side of the space. Ezra picked one and ascended it, Claudia close behind. A corridor lined with doors was at the top of the stairs. He opened the second on the left. "The blue rooms," he announced.

She stepped inside and gasped. "Oh, my." The room's wallpaper was sky blue, printed with tiny clouds. The ceiling was painted a matching shade, a large round yellow electric light hanging from it. She guessed it was supposed to look like the sun. In the middle of the room was an enormous canopied bed, the curtains blue and white, tied on the bed posts with ribbons. The covers were plush, blankets and pillows piled high. Her luggage was waiting for her in front of a wooden wardrobe painted in a pastel rainbow of colors. "This is beautiful! Julian said there's more than one blue room?"

Ezra nodded. "It's joined to this one." He crossed the

room to open a door that she hadn't noticed. It was papered, too, blending in with the wall. Curious, she followed him.

Where her room was bright and sunny, his was dark. This room was decorated with deep blue paper flecked with gold and silver stars. Silver and gold stars were strung from the ceiling, surrounding a hanging white globe. The bed matched the one in Claudia's room, save for the bedding a darker blue. "Oh, this is lovely, too!" she exclaimed. She made a beeline for the bed, wanting to see if it was as soft as it looked. She collapsed on it to look at the black and blue lacy canopy overhead. "Did Julian decorate the rooms? They seem too tasteful for him to have done this."

"No, this was his parents' doing. I think."

She levered herself up on her elbows to better look at him. He stood at the side of the bed, an unreadable expression on his face. "Where are they?"

"They live abroad."

"So, he just rattles around this big house all alone?" Saying the words sent pangs of loneliness through her. She had nearly gone mad from it when she was still a ghost.

"Julian doesn't lack for company."

Claudia thought about the lascivious way his gaze had raked her form. The man had a certain magnetism about him, even if she wasn't particularly attracted to him. She hadn't been desired in over a thousand years. It was a heady feeling to know someone thought of her that way after all this time. "I suppose he isn't married, then?"

A shadow crossed over Ezra's face. It was gone so quickly that Claudia thought she must have imagined it. "No," he replied. "I would have been invited to the wedding, I think."

That reminded Claudia of something she'd been

curious about since she moved in with him. "Why aren't you married?" Was it her imagination, or did he color at her words?

"It hasn't happened."

She hauled herself to a seated position. "Why not? People were married when they were children when I was a girl."

His eyes widened. "That's horrifying. That's also happened here, but not for a long time."

"I was nearly married when I was a girl." She hasn't meant to say the words. It wasn't a memory she looked upon fondly.

He looked stricken. "I'm so sorry."

"It didn't happen. The man I was supposed to marry at first died in a quarry accident, I think. It's been so long that I don't remember anymore. I was secretly relieved I didn't have to marry him, but pretended to be upset for the sake of my parents. They liked him." She was babbling. It was a habit she'd had since the first time she was alive when she was nervous or couldn't read a situation. If she didn't stop talking, she would bring up the second man she had been arranged to marry, the reason she died in the first place, and she wasn't ready for that conversation.

It was Ezra that was causing it. Ezra's face when she asked about Julian. Sad and somehow ... hurt? That was silly. Ezra could have any mistress or wife he wanted. He was still young and had a sizable fortune bolstering him. As it was the first time she was alive, those features were desirable in a husband.

Ezra hesitated before asking, "You said hat you were engaged before ... well, *before*. You didn't marry at all?"

In all their months together, sharing his home and meals and their mutual grief, he had never asked such a question. Claudia had never volunteered that kind of information, either. She supposed they'd been through enough together that she could be honest. "No, we didn't make it to the altar." She regretted the words as soon as she said them. It had been over a thousand years since her death, but she still wasn't ready to talk about Marcus.

Something in her voice must have told Ezra not to prod further, because he merely nodded. "I'm sorry."

"For what?"

"That you didn't get to see through marrying your fiancé."

While Ezra was often caustic with others, he'd always been sensitive and gentle with her. From the time she materialized in that parlor, freshly resurrected, he had always been there for her. According to Merritt and Ivy, he'd never behaved that way around anyone. Here he was, trying to make her feel better about an engagement to a man who betrayed her in the worst possible way. Who didn't know that she'd followed Marcus from Londinium to what eventually became Liverpool after she died.

"It was for the best that it didn't happen," she replied. "I prefer being alive in the nineteenth century to the fourth."

Ezra opened his mouth to speak, only to be interrupted by a knock at the door. "Supper's waiting," called Julian from the other side. "Get out of your traveling clothes and come back downstairs." He snickered.

Ezra sighed, as if he knew what was coming next.

"Unless you're already out of them."

Claudia bit back a smile. Ezra remained stony-faced. She'd forgotten about the upper-class custom of changing into special clothes for meals. She rose from the bed. "I won't be long," she said, heading for the door that separated their rooms.

"Neither will I," he replied.

Once in her room, she opened her luggage, and surveyed the available clothes. As she changed into her favorite trousers, she wondered about Ezra's emotional distance, his odd questions. Perhaps it was time to tell him more of who she really was, the reason she'd haunted the mortal plane as long as she had.

CHAPTER 4

IT WAS NEARING MIDNIGHT, Julian's party in full swing in a room he described as a grotto. The only thing grotto-like was the humidity, Ezra noted, thanks to the giant glass tank filled with blue-dyed water in the middle of the room. A gramophone played a wax cylinder of an annoyingly upbeat song Ezra was unfamiliar with, the sound crackly and irritating to his ears. He tried to tune it out as he nursed his wine, his second of the evening. He needed to remain as sober as possible for Claudia's sake. He was relieved to see she followed suit, taking occasional sips from a glass of wine. She stayed at his side, another relief, especially with the interest she had drawn from the other guests. Ezra hadn't brought a guest to a party since they were at university, preferring to keep his business with his mistresses separate as he got older. He'd introduced everyone to Claudia, who politely nodded at each and let the men kiss the back of her hand in drunken, melodramatic fashion.

There was Isaac Palfrey, of course, perhaps the most notorious of their circle, someone who would never turn down a drink. There was Hester Phillips, *nee* Randolph, on the arm of the husband she'd met while learning to paint. Her husband had been a nude life model, Hester the artist he'd immediately been taken with. A decade of marriage clearly hadn't dimmed their ardor for each other, judging from the way they were entwined on a velvet brocade chaise. Even though they were still dressed, Ezra turned away to give them some privacy.

When he glanced at Claudia next to him, her cheeks were pink.

Arthur and Adelaide McCabe, twins with remarkable industrial design skills, were talking with Theodore Redfield, a middling art student who had ended up in the sales side of the gallery world. Theo listened with amusement as the twins stumbled over their words, trying to describe the patterned carpets they had designed together and were about to go into mass production. They kept interrupting each other, sometimes accusing the other of having no business sense, a comedic act they'd inadvertently perfected since their first-year courses. Theo looked ready to step away, but every time he tried to pull himself away, Arthur grabbed his shirtsleeve. "Have you considered getting into the mass production business?" he asked, not for the first time. His words slurred together. "Everyone wants something pretty in their house these days and not everyone can set out a hundred quid for a piece."

Conspicuously absent was Eugene Moore, now living in Italy and married to a countess, and Victoria Pickford, who was apparently expecting her second child any day now with her industrialist husband. Ezra thought he might have liked to catch up with both of them, but supposed a letter would have to suffice later.

In another part of the room, Julian held court with a couple of women Ezra introduced to him as nieces of one of Julian's patrons. He racked his brain, trying to recall their names and came up short. He took a generous swallow of wine, noting he was nearly at the bottom of his glass, as he looked around the room, trying to figure out where he belonged now. He'd been gone from London for so long, had stalled his career while indulging in every other pleasure. At least Julian and everyone else here could balance art and debauchery.

The water in the tank rippled as its gas heaters sent up a blast of warmth at the base. When he glanced at Claudia, he saw a curious look on her face, reminiscent of the time at the market when she climbed into a pen of sheepdog puppies for sale to play with them. "Don't even think about it," he murmured in her ear.

"Oh, I'm thinking about it, but I can't get in there with all these people around," she whispered back.

Her breath tickled the sensitive skin under his ear, sending an unexpected bolt of heat through him. He shivered, then hoped she didn't notice. "It's hardly big enough for one person," he said.

"What does Julian want to do with it?"

"I'm not sure. All I can say is that you shouldn't get in that tank, because the water is already going off. Julian's going to have a mold problem if he doesn't take care of it."

"My ears are burning." The man at the center of their conversation sidled over to Ezra and Claudia. His voice was deep and loose from drink. His eyes were red-rimmed but otherwise alert. "It's rude to talk about someone right in front of them."

"The water tank," Claudia said helpfully.

"Oh, it's a bit of an eyesore, isn't it? I'd planned to fill it with aquatic plants, but it turns out England is somewhat lacking in them. Except for the seaweed, I suppose, but I don't want to paw through the Thames to bring some back." Julian shuddered faintly.

"I'm not certain that's seaweed," Ezra replied.

"Whatever it is, I don't want it in my house anymore after the party. I'm going to get rid of the tank once I find someone to take it off my hands. It's from a Liverpool warehouse once owned by my father's late cousin, actually. Perhaps it wants to come back with you?" Julian gave Ezra a hopeful expression.

"You've seen my flat. Where the hell would I put a water tank?"

Julian shrugged. "Perhaps you'd like a larger bathtub?"

Claudia giggled at that answer, drawing a smile from Julian.

His attention fixed on her, he asked, "How are you enjoying yourself? You've been stuck to Ezra like a burr all evening. It's selfish of him to keep you to himself."

Ezra's breath caught. Dimly, he was aware of one of Julian's lady friends resetting the gramophone, playing that blasted song again from the beginning. "She's a trifle shy," Ezra said quickly.

"We're all friendly here," Julian assured them. He looked over his shoulder at Hester and her husband. The buttons on her blouse were half undone. "Some of us are a little too friendly," he said, voice rising. It caught the attention of her and her husband, both of whom had the grace to color. They sat and Hester straightened her clothes. Julian grinned.

"You have a very unique house," Claudia finally said. Her shoulders stiffened, her expression shifting as she tried to suppress a yawn. Ezra knew that expression, how the shadows under her eyes would only get deeper as the evening drew on. She was exhausted.

"I've certainly tried. My work keeps my neighbors on

their toes. Can I get either of you another drink?" Julian glanced around the room, although if he was looking for a servant or an open bottle somewhere, Ezra couldn't tell.

"No, thank you," he quickly replied. Glancing at Claudia, he added, "I think we'll be taking our leave shortly, anyway. It's been a long day."

"Taking your leave? You mean, going upstairs?" Julian wiggled his eyebrows in a way that Ezra guessed was supposed to be suggestive, but it came off as ridiculous.

"Yes, upstairs. To sleep." Ezra's tone was sharper than he'd intended, not wanting to get into a war of innuendo with his friend. A fleeting image of himself and Claudia ascending the stairs to the blue room crossed his mind. In it, she wore a heated look and her nightgown, her hand wrapped in his, skin hot. He fought the urge to pull at his collar, even though the room's humidity would have provided an explanation for such a motion.

What the hell was wrong with him? He shouldn't be seeing Claudia in that light.

A small voice reminded him that he already had, quite a few times in recent weeks, an attraction he ignored. He cared for her in a way he'd never bothered to about anyone else, that was all. He hadn't had any sort of romantic entanglements since she came into his life, and was feeling deprived. It was something he could rectify if he could be bothered to seek out a companion.

Claudia drained her glass, then left it on a fussy little wooden table crowded with empty drinkware, red wine stains dried in the bottoms. "I could use some rest." She curled her arm around Ezra's and turned dark eyes up at him. "Thank you for the lovely evening," she said to Julian.

Julian took her free hand and kissed it. Ezra tamped down an expected flare of jealousy.

"It was my pleasure, madam. And this is hardly the

evening that will be the talk of London. Just wait until tomorrow. I'll have costumes sent to your room tomorrow night for the party after the exhibition opening. I picked all of them myself."

Oh, no. Ezra hadn't even considered that Julian would have some kind of stupid dress code, although in retrospect, he should have. "We'll argue over the costumes tomorrow." Julian grinned, and Ezra knew that whatever they were, they were going to be ridiculous.

"Have a good night, Julian," Claudia said politely.

"I plan to, even if you two insist on going to bed at such an early hour. If you're awake before the rest of us in the morning, the cook left some food in the icebox for early risers. He won't start cooking hot food until at least ten o'clock, on my instruction."

At last, they finally left the grotto. The change in humidity was immediate when the door closed behind them. Claudia turned her tired gaze up to him. "Thank you," she murmured, before briefly leaning against him.

The frankincense scent of her hair met him. He let himself enjoy the fragrance for a scant second before replying. "What for?"

"It's a lot in there," she said quietly. She nodded her head at the closed door.

The gramophone's volume increased, the noise enhanced with Arthur singing along, voice off-key. "I'd like to say that they aren't always like that, but it would be a lie." They strolled along the corridor. It was dark save for the light offered by electric wall sconces. The artwork on the walls looked more ominous, the painted figures looking demonic instead of pleasured.

"Are you like that? When I'm not with you?"

"I was, although not quite like Julian is tonight." The staircase in the marbled foyer was thankfully better lit than the rest of the house. They still took care ascending the stairs. "It feels like he's trying too hard," Ezra admitted before he could reconsider his words.

"How so? Isn't this kind of celebration expected with your artist friends?"

"Perhaps when we were still in university. It feels like he's clinging to his youth, I suppose."

Once on the landing, Claudia halted. Her voice was an indignant whisper. "You're still young! All of you are!"

"So are you," he replied, confused.

"I'm one thou …" She paused, then lowered her voice again. "I'm over a thousand years old. Fifteen hundred! I'm positively ancient. Anyway, I'm not going to argue that point with you." She looked around them, at the landings and stairs that branched off in separate directions. "Are we turning right or left for our rooms?"

"Left."

"I thought so, but I can't tell that well in the dark." Without letting go of his arm, she let him lead her to the wing where the blue rooms were.

Outside their doors, Ezra paused. "I've left the door between our rooms unlocked," he said.

"I doubt I'll have to bother you." Her full lips turned up. Not for the first time, he wondered what they tasted like.

"Good night, Ezra."

To his shock, she leaned up and pressed a chaste kiss to his cheek. He felt it as acutely as if he'd been branded. The sensation nearly made him stumble back. When he found his voice, all he could say was, "Sleep well."

She twisted the handle on her bedroom door and stepped inside. "I will."

～

THE SKY WAS STILL gray with a poor excuse for the dawn when Claudia woke up and peeked through the curtains. It was free of air traffic, at least from what she could see, compared to Liverpool's near-constant buzzing of ornithopters at all hours, or perhaps it was only because of the wealthy neighborhood. The streets were nearly empty, too, save for a single steam cab that ambled along.

Her stomach rumbled as she gazed outside, reminding her why she was awake in the first place. Hadn't Julian mentioned last night that there would be cold foodstuffs in the kitchen for early risers? Claudia dug through the pile of clothing crammed in her luggage, pulling out her woolen wrap and a pair of socks. After she had draped herself with it, she left the room, looking on either side of the corridor to see if there were any other guests up. Her footsteps were muffled by the thick carpet under her feet.

It was Julian she didn't want to cross paths with, she realized.

Julian didn't seem a bad sort, just … petulant. Immature. She didn't like how his gaze raked over her, like he was appraising a sculpture instead of speaking to a person. It was hard to believe that he and Ezra had been friends for so long.

She traced her steps back to the empty kitchen and opened the enormous icebox. Plates had already been prepared, covered with small copper domes. Lifting one, she found sliced ham and boiled eggs beneath. Ham and eggs weren't her favorite, but they would do for today. She removed a plate, and after considering it for a few seconds, took out another. Ezra might well be awake now, or nearly awake. He was often up shortly after her, although she suspected it was because he worried about her flooding the kitchen or setting something on fire.

Fire hadn't terrified her as much as she thought it

would, oddly enough. The sight of flames didn't bother her as much as the smell of smoke. Closing her eyes, Claudia willed away her last memories from before she died. She breathed deeply until the images left, replaced by Ezra's coolly handsome visage. She'd kissed him last night, she recalled. Her whole body heated at the memory, mercifully replacing her anxiety. She didn't know what had possessed her to do such a thing, chaste as it was. Perhaps it was the wine that made her do it. He'd just looked so forlorn, so defeated, and she hated to see him that way.

Not trusting herself to navigate the house with plates in both hands, she dug through the kitchen cabinets, finding a stack of identical silver trays. They were tarnished from disuse, but they would do. Out of curiosity, Claudia counted them. Twenty in all. Her eyes widened. Once upon a time, Julian's parents must have held incredible parties. Hopefully ones without giant stinking water tanks, too. She shuddered at the memory of the humidity and smell.

She carried the tray back to her room, setting the tray on a polished wooden table near the window, flanked by a pair of chairs. She hesitated in front of the door that joined their rooms before gently knocking. An unexpected swarm of butterflies took up residence in her stomach as she waited. This was *Ezra* she was waiting for, after all. No reason to be nervous around her closest friend.

Finally, she heard shuffling on the other side, and the door opened, revealing a sleepy Ezra. His blond hair stuck up in all directions around his head, dressing gown loosely tied around his waist. She had seen him in the morning before, but rarely like this: disheveled and half-asleep. He was always so put together, hardly ever leaving his bedroom unless he was dressed. Unlike Claudia, who had no issue with lounging around his flat in her nightwear.

"I brought breakfast, if you want some."

He blinked, considering her words. "All right."

Claudia stepped away from the door, holding it open. He shuffled to the table where she'd left the trays, Claudia trailing behind him. "Did I wake you?"

He shrugged. "I've been tossing and turning all night."

Guilt threaded through her, replacing the butterflies in her belly with a hard ball of anxiety. "You could go back to sleep."

"Later, perhaps." He managed a smile before lifting a dome off his plate.

"What time does the exhibit start?" Claudia asked after she uncovered her own meal. She wished she had some chocolate, something sweet to accompany it.

"Officially six o'clock, but I'm certain Julian and everyone will start their party beforehand." He sounded a little despondent at the prospect.

"Did you used to behave like that? Drink yourself into oblivion?" Claudia cut a piece of ham and ate it. Ugh. She really didn't care for meat that much.

"But of course. That's what's expected of an ingrate with too much family money behind him. I suppose I've grown up in a way the others haven't yet, except perhaps Victoria."

There hadn't been a Victoria present last night to the best of Claudia's memory. An unexpected flash of jealousy flared in her at the mention of the woman's name. She tamped it down, forced herself to keep her voice even. "Who is she?"

If Ezra noticed anything about her shift in mood, he didn't let on. "One of our friends, one of the few of us who is married, a child on the way last I heard. A proper adult, I suppose."

Claudia relaxed a little. "I see."

"I'm more concerned about the after party, to be honest with you," Ezra confessed. He leaned back in his chair, breakfast seemingly forgotten. "Well, I'm concerned about the whole affair."

"But you two are friends," she protested.

"We are. We're different people now. Julian has figured out who he is, I think, and I ..." He trailed off and looked out the window, although Claudia knew he wasn't focusing on anything in particular. "I'm not sure."

Her heartbeat unexpectedly picked up speed. With breakfast forgotten, she leaned forward a little. "What do you mean?"

"I'm not certain who I am." He spoke the words thoughtfully, as if he was tasting them for the first time. "I've spent my years since university acting the stereotypical self-indulgent artist, without the art."

Claudia knew that Ezra had already shown sides of himself to her that hadn't to anyone else. She'd done much the same with him. But this moment of vulnerability, his voice sounding almost ashamed at ... what, exactly? Not having a gargantuan house to rattle around in, surrounded by lewd paintings and a giant water tank that served no purpose other than to stink? "You've realized you're unhappy with the way your life is moving," she said gently.

"Yes." He gave her a look she couldn't identify, but it summoned the same butterfly squadron that had taken up residence in her belly earlier. It was a look meant for only her.

It took Claudia a few seconds to find her voice. "What changed?"

There was a rough undercurrent to his voice. "You already know that it's you."

A strange thrill coursed through her at the admission.

"Looking after you forced me to think about someone

other than myself. I've never had any siblings nor cousins, aside from Ivy's family that I've only met a time or two. You're the reason the world stopped revolving around me."

Claudia's breath caught and her muscles froze for a moment at his earnestness. She had seen him in softer moments before, when he'd spoke of his regret about his relationship with his father and Ivy. His father communicating with him from beyond the grave the night they met had rattled him to his core, the effect still obvious months later. He'd never spoken of regrets in the present, of things he could already change. "I see," she finally murmured. She wanted to confess something to him as well, open herself up in the same way he had. All she could think of was telling him how she died, and that was the last thing she wanted to think about right now even though he probably deserved to know. A part of her itched to tell him and finally have it off her chest; another, logical part of her knew it would color the entire London trip. She didn't want his memories of his friend's art exhibition to be the same dismal gray as the city skies. Her bringing up her own death couldn't be distilled to a sentence or two about learning not to be selfish.

Something else about his statement pulled at her. "What happens after I move on? Will you return to being the sun the Earth revolves around?"

His brows lifted. "I take umbrage with both of those statements. First, where are you planning on going, and second, where did you learn about astronomy?"

"A former tenant in the flat across the corridor from Merritt's enjoyed astronomy as a hobby. I listened." She shrugged.

"In between haunting him?"

"I did not haunt." She eyed him archly. A small smile lifted the corner of his mouth, an expression that relieved her to see. "I shared mortal-built spaces with humans on this plane. Haunting implies that I tried to frighten people." Even though she hadn't done those things, tenants in that flat tended to leave rather quickly. Apparently, she had a faint frankincense scent that was discernible even to those without fae ancestors or necromancy ability, according to Merritt.

"I defer to your expertise. You didn't answer my more important question. Are you planning on moving on?" There was an odd tightness to his voice.

"I don't have immediate plans to, as long as you're comfortable with me living in your spare room, but what if your life changes? What if you get married?"

A shadow crossed his features. "Marriage hadn't crossed my mind."

"I'm certain it will someday soon. You're getting on in years. You're nearly thirty. Aren't most people married by that age these days?"

"Ah, yes, I'd forgotten that you were engaged when you were a child. And you've forgotten that you told me as recently as last night that I'm hardly old."

"I was betrothed, and there was a difference between those states. That betrothal was broken, anyway." Interest flickered across his face at that bit of information, as it always did whenever she mentioned her old life. "It's customary now to marry when one is an adult."

"I haven't maintained a mistress nor entertained any companions since last year, so no, I don't have any designs on marriage at the moment. I like that you live with me, Claudia. You know you're welcome as long as you want to be there. I'd miss you if you left."

"I'd miss you, too."

Ezra's gaze was soft, and for a moment she thought he had more to say. "We need tea."

She hadn't been expecting that. "I didn't look for the kettle in the kitchen."

"There's bound to be at least three in there. Let's look." He stood.

"But you're not dressed."

"No one will care if they've even woken up from their drunken stupors yet. If I cannot sleep in an unfamiliar bed, the least I can do is get some caffeine into me." He took her arm, a gesture she would never tire of. "Let's look."

CHAPTER 5

EZRA HAD ASSUMED Julian's exhibition would be held at a gallery adjacent to their university, one of the smaller venues that dealt with new French-inspired artwork, or even a wing of the South Kensington Museum. How foolish he had been. The gallery was located in a converted ship, rudder and propellers removed that barely bobbed along the Thames where she was docked, but it was disconcerting all the same. Perhaps it was the persistent odor that wafted from the river water, the stench of a thousand years. He took a deep breath, centering himself before pasting a smile on his face. He was here to celebrate his friend's achievement, bizarre as it was.

The marble sculpture before him was flawless in a technical sense, its proportions that of an ordinary human woman, the folds of her skirt pooling around her feet. Carved bare toes peeked out from beneath its hem. Her face bore an inscrutable expression, eyes closed as if she was asleep, making the viewer guess as to whether or not she was pleased about nursing the baby pig she held to her bare breast. Ezra thought about Julian's earlier remarks about Roman sculpture's influence on his work. He could sort of see it, although he couldn't recall the last time he saw marble statues of ladies nursing livestock.

There were other sculptures in similar styles arranged around the room, which looked to be a first-class ballroom in the ship's previous life. A granite couple wearing formal evening clothes but with the faces of horses had gathered a few people, all of whom quietly exclaimed over how they could look posed in their gardens. Ezra didn't know how much the statues were selling for and wasn't gauche enough to ask. Based on the attire and accents of the patrons, they were moneyed enough.

Another section of the ship was devoted to paintings, mostly tempera on wood. They weren't as vulgar as Julian's old Hieronymus Bosch tributes installed in his home, instead almost matching the statues in the ballroom. They depicted ordinary domestic scenes out of history, with the painted figures appearing bored or hesitant, sometimes fearful. He examined one large piece of a group of French aristocrats gathered around a table on a palace balcony, their cat heads topped with high white wigs, as a cluster of people painted as mice looked up at a guillotine under construction on the ground. It was big enough that it would take up nearly an entire wall in his flat. For the first time, terror struck Ezra. Was he expected to buy one of Julian's pieces? Would his friend be offended if he didn't find a home for a statue of a nude figure with the face of a sheep? Where the hell would he display such a thing?

"There you are."

Ezra started before turning around to see Victoria Pickford. Once upon a time, the sight would have made his pulse quicken and added a stutter to his voice, but he'd long moved on from his infatuation with her.

She was still beautiful, her reddish-brown hair artfully

arranged around her head in some kind of coronet style. Her blue gown was subtly adorned with tiny paste jewels that sparkled in the electric lights arranged around the room. Her belly gave credence to the talk that she was pregnant.

"I'm surprised to see you here tonight, Victoria."

She smiled, revealing even white teeth. "I could say the same about you. There's a bigger turnout tonight than I thought there would be." She placed a hand on her stomach.

"I didn't think you would want to travel in your condition," Ezra replied.

"We're only in Twickenham, hardly a journey. We could use a quick trip to London before the baby arrives." She spoke frankly about her pregnancy, which Ezra appreciated. She had never been one for euphemisms in polite society.

He mentally corrected himself. His group of university friends could hardly be considered polite society despite their moneyed and aristocratic upbringings. "When are you expecting the baby's debut?"

"Debut, I like that. Perhaps a month?" Victoria gave a half-shrug. She looked around the room at the other patrons to see if they were listening. Her voice dropped. "I'm looking forward to this being over. No one tells you how much your back and hips hurt, or how uncomfortable it is to sleep. I'll be very happy to hold the baby in my arms instead of my body."

Ezra wasn't sure how to answer that. "Congratulations, all the same."

"What about you?" she asked.

"No by-blows yet."

She smiled at the quip. "What about your lovely companion? Julian pointed her out when I boarded the ship."

Ezra's heart fluttered. Whether it was the thought of Claudia or the implication that they were a couple, he couldn't say. "Where is she?" he asked. Panic threaded through him at the thought that she might have gone overboard. He was being ridiculous. If anyone had fallen off the ship's deck, he would have heard the screams from the assembled crowd first.

"Julian was bending her ear in front of the horse statue."

"Which one?" The question slipped out before Ezra could politely excuse himself and find her. Which was also ridiculous, because Claudia was an adult. One relatively new to the modern world, but an adult all the same. It was good that she was speaking to people other than himself.

"The gentleman horse with the intricately detailed chest hair." Victoria's lips thinned as she tried to keep herself from giggling.

For some reason, Ezra felt the need to defend Julian's work, bizarre as it was. "He really did put on a good show," he said, looking around the space again. "The patrons seem to appreciate his work."

"It certainly makes a statement."

"It took a lot to pull this off."

"Possible. You *do* remember who his relations are, don't you? His father is one of the most prominent patrons of the Tate Britain and his aunt is chairwoman of the second largest artists' colony in the country. He had help." She lowered her voice. "You could have done this if you wanted."

"Ah, yes. All of my connections I have from my father's patent medicine legacy."

"I mean your work. You could have a big exhibition like this."

"Doubtful. Landscapes and dour portraiture don't pull the same demand as a woman nursing a piglet." All of a sudden, he wished he had a drink in hand. "I don't really miss it."

"You've stopped your artwork altogether?" Victoria looked aghast at the notion.

Ezra tried not to let irritation color his words. "I'm an artist of middling talent and even lower motivation. And you're one to speak about giving up. When was the last time you stood at an easel?"

"That's different. Charles and I work in design. You know that. I'm still working as an artist, just a different kind. There's just as much to do with wallpaper patterns as painting a river." She gave a pointed look at one of the paintings. "Or a man with a tiger tail." She moved a few steps closer to the piece, squinting at it. "Oh, my. I think the tail is on the front."

"I don't think it's a tail."

She stepped away, a blush touching her cheeks. "Neither do I."

Ezra grinned. It was rare to see someone as unflappable as Victoria have that kind of reaction to artwork. "At least it isn't a clockwork penis. He made vague threats about them when he met us at the train station."

Victoria sputtered, trying to contain her laughter. "This is a trifle more mature, but not by much." She smiled and sighed. "I'm pleased to see you settled down, Ezra."

"I haven't …" It took a few seconds for him to parse out her meaning. "Oh, you mean Claudia. We're not a couple." Something in him twisted at the admission, an odd pain he'd never experienced. He didn't like it.

Victoria pinned him with a curious stare. "I see."

"Men and women can't be friends?"

"Of course they can be. My apologies for assuming.

You just seemed so, I don't know, *defensive* when I mentioned her speaking with Julian. You had this odd little wrinkle between your eyebrows."

"Julian chases after anyone he finds attractive." The words slipped out before Ezra could stop himself.

"So do you."

The conversation was taking a turn he didn't want to go down. "Not anymore," he replied tightly. "Claudia and Julian are free to speak to whomever they want." An image of Julian leading Claudia away by the hand popped into his mind, unwelcome and unsettling. Ezra's hands curled into fists at the notion, and he had to force himself to relax.

Something shifted in Victoria's expression, like she had just discovered something about Ezra. "Why don't you tell her how you feel?"

"She's my friend. She already knows that. I think she might be my best friend, actually." Ezra surprised himself with that last statement. He'd never had a best friend before, never felt the need for one.

Victoria gave him a look that said she didn't believe him but didn't argue further. "I'm glad to see you have a best friend, then."

Claudia appeared in the sculpture gallery, hair a little windblown as if she had been wandering around the deck outside. Her dark eyes scanned the room, settling on Ezra with a smile before quickly crossing the room to meet him. "I've been looking for … oh, is that a tail?" Her gaze caught the painting.

Victoria hid a smile behind a manicured hand.

"I think it's up to the viewer to decide what it is," Ezra replied.

Claudia turned a bright smile to Victoria. "Hello."

Remembering his manners, Ezra introduced them. "Victoria and I attended university together."

"Are you an artist, too?" she asked.

"I'm an industrial designer. Wallpaper patterns, that sort of thing."

Any reply Claudia might have had was cut off by the ship rocking back and forth. Victoria fell against the wall, crashing into the tiger tail painting, Ezra to the floor. Claudia barely managed to keep her footing. There were other crashes to the floor from the other guests. "What the hell?" muttered Ezra. Around him, he heard similar sentiments. He quickly regained his footing, half expecting the ship to lurch again. "Are you two all right?" he asked, looking at each of them in turn.

Victoria patted her belly. "Baby and I are just fine. What was that?"

Claudia looked like she had something to say, but thought better of it. Her lips thinned before she answered. "I'm all right, too."

"Did Julian tell you he was going to set off fireworks or something? I wouldn't put it past him to pull a stunt like that." Ezra looked around the gallery for his friend.

"Do you really think he would try to blow something up on a boat?" Claudia asked.

"Yes," Ezra and Victoria replied in unison.

The subject of their conversation burst into the gallery. "I don't know what that was, but the effect was much better when I was reading from that book," he announced. His voice was deep and loose, a sure sign that he'd already had plenty to drink.

Claudia's brows raised, making Ezra wonder what exactly Julian had been reciting on the lower deck. Ezra sighed as Julian approached them. "What book?" he asked.

An older woman wearing a velvet gown that was a touch too formal for the occasion approached him. "Mr.

Smythe, the use of color in *Dastardly* is simply remarkable," she purred.

Julian forgot what he was going to say to them in favor of praise. He turned a winning smile to her. "It warms the cockles of my heart to hear that, my lady."

She waved a gloved hand at the honorific. "My dear boy, call me Amelia in these settings. I'm here strictly as an art lover. My husband and I will be putting in an offer for it tonight. It would make the perfect conversation piece for our guest cottage." Her eyes narrowed. "You haven't sold it yet, have you?"

"Of course not. *Dastardly* has been waiting for you since I daubed the last feather."

"Wonderful! I'll have to tell the Peckinghams they've lost out on it, then." She beamed at Julian. "Such a lovely evening so far, aside from that portside upset. What happened?"

Julian shrugged. "Your guess is as good as mine. You know how unpredictable the water can be. I was reading from a book I picked up in a shop a while back, and that happened. Rather eerie, actually, the book is supposed to be a bunch of old curses and whatnot."

Ezra's blood ran cold. He knew the power incantations could have in the right circumstances. It was the reason Claudia stood beside him today, the reason his father had been able to communicate with him from beyond the grave. In that moment, he dearly wished that Merritt Sloan, his stepmother's new husband who was familiar with dark magic, was here. It couldn't be a coincidence that the boat was rocked while Julian recited an old curse or spell.

Oh, my God, Julian, what have you done?

He caught Claudia's eye. The stricken expression on her face told him she had the same suspicions he did.

But Merritt and Ivy were in Spain, last he heard. He knew no one else with magical abilities. If Julian had summoned something or broken a vital part of the universe, none of them had any idea how to set it to rights. How was he to bring up the subject to Julian without sounding insane?

Any concern Julian might have had about what just happened was clearly obliterated by alcohol and his own need for praise. To the lady, he asked, "Amelia, will you and Lord Folkestone be joining me at my home after the gallery closes?"

Victoria rolled her eyes at the question but didn't comment.

Amelia playfully batted him on the arm. "Of course not. I don't participate in debauchery at my age. I merely patronize those who do."

Julian looked at the rest of them. "Ezra and Claudia, I expect your attendance. Victoria, what about you and Charles?"

"You can't be serious." Victoria patted her belly again.

The ship rocked again, a little more gently this time, but disconcerting all the same. Outside the porthole, a flash of light streaked across the night sky. Ezra and Claudia both reached out to steady Victoria.

"Certainly memorable," Julian commented.

For all the wrong reasons. With a sinking feeling of dread, Ezra couldn't help but think about what kind of hell Julian might have accidentally unleashed. *No*, he reminded himself. *Julian doesn't have any magical abilities, not like Merritt or Ivy. Regular people can't cast spells and summon things.*

He took another look at Claudia, who appeared as tense as he felt. He tried to give her what he hoped was a reassuring smile.

Can they?

CHAPTER 6

IT SEEMED like half of the people crowding the moored boat had been invited back to Julian's house for a party. Everyone was herded into cabs rented for the occasion for the trek back, including Claudia and Ezra. Unfortunately, that meant that there was little opportunity for her to speak to Ezra about what she overheard before the incident aboard the ship.

She had grown bored aboard the ship listening to Julian talk about his work and discreetly slipped out the open door to the deck for fresh air. The Thames had been as cold as she remembered the last time she was in Londinium, hundreds of years ago, making her glad she'd brought a fine woolen wrap with her at Ezra's suggestion. As she gazed out at the water—certainly filthier and smellier than it had been in the fourth century—she idly wondered what had become of the witch who read her fortune shortly before she died. Witches were always beautiful, she recalled. Ivy definitely was. It was the first thing about her that had distracted Merritt when Ezra hired him to investigate his father's death. Would she be able to find the approximate place the witch's tent had been? Or her family's home, for that matter?

"The seller said it was curses."

Julian's voice had boomed out across the ship's lower deck, through the door, snapping Claudia to attention. She moved away from the railing to return to the gathering inside. Julian held a small, leather-bound book in his hand that he used to gesture with. "I said I didn't care, and for half a shilling, the curses can't be that potent. I used some of the pages to mix into plaster for this piece. I call it 'The Curse' in homage to it." He gently traced his free hand over the curves of a sculpture that looked like a person hunched over into itself. Its back showed raised vertebrae, speckled with bits of paper.

Claudia looked away and rolled her eyes.

Julian continued. "They're so melodramatic, too. *Ego oriri iube malum.* I looked up the translation. How generic can a fellow be with his curses?" He accepted a glass of something amber-colored from a liveried servant and took a healthy swallow.

Claudia stilled at the use of the Latin language, butchered as it was. "I command mischief to rise" wasn't a particularly grim phrase to utter, and she agreed that it was certainly melodramatic. It took her a few seconds to realize what had changed.

The air.

The air felt off, like it was spoiling. It had to be the river causing her to feel this way, she decided. It was a combination of being on the Thames and the wine she had sipped while Julian talked her ear off. Air didn't spoil.

"*Surge inferum,*" Julian added, laughing, then tucked the book away in his coat pocket. "Ridiculous."

Claudia wouldn't consider a command for hell to rise from the earth ridiculous, given what she had seen through the centuries. Her resurrection was proof enough of the power of words. She had left the deck, needing to find Ezra to tell him what she heard, hear from him that Julian probably hadn't done anything stupid. When she found him, she'd been too distracted by remembering her manners with his friends to discreetly pull him away, and then the ship started lurching. She had stayed at his side, but Julian followed them as they left the ship and boarded the vehicles that would bring them back to his weird, brass tile-covered house.

Damnation.

She couldn't ask Ezra if they could retreat back to his townhouse. Anywhere but Julian's home. Even the prospect of returning to the beautiful blue rooms no longer held appeal. Regret at the Londinium trip set in. She was squeezed between Ezra and Julian aboard a rattling tin can of a steam cab.

Julian blathered on about a piece that had broken, how he wouldn't let it spoil his gallery show. Based on the way he kept repeating that he wasn't upset, Claudia suspected that might be a lie.

She leaned closer to Ezra in a feeble attempt to move away from Julian. Across from them, three other patrons whose names Claudia had forgotten hung on to Julian's every word.

"An undertow!" Julian raged. "How the hell could an undertow shake the ship like that? It boggles the mind!"

Claudia held back a sigh of irritation.

"I thought the fireworks were part of the show," one of the women said.

Claudia had already forgotten her name.

"That wasn't a firework. I don't have a clue what that was," Julian griped.

Ezra looked down at Claudia, blue eyes wide. He was

probably remembering the streak of light racing across the sky.

It had reminded her of a shooting star, albeit one that shot off in the wrong direction. She wished they were alone to put their heads together, figure out what happened. No, she wished Merritt or Ivy were here, too. They would know what the hell had happened.

"You did make some sales, Jules," the woman said reassuringly. "And there were all those reporters and critics, too. They seemed very pleased with your work."

Julian grunted in response. "Not all the critics were there and it was still cut short."

"Surely you can have another showing. There's bound to be more interest when reviews hit the papers over the next few days."

"It's all to be moved off the ship for safety purposes next week. It won't have the same impact on land," Julian replied sullenly.

Ugh, what a brat. Claudia turned back to Ezra and tried to convey that in the look she sent his way. He gave her a tight smile and squeezed her gloved hand. Unexpected warmth flooded her, making her wish there wasn't any material between their skin. She felt herself flush at the thought. It wasn't the first time she'd felt that way, but those notions had been steadily increasing in recent weeks. It was unsettling, and she couldn't decide if she liked the feeling or not.

"At least there's a party to look forward to," Julian said, although didn't sound particularly excited. He turned his head to Claudia and Ezra. "I meant what I said about a dress code. Your costumes were placed on your beds by the servants during the exhibition."

"Oh, God," muttered Ezra.

"Nothing too indecent. I just wanted to keep the theme

of unexpected debauchery continuing through the evening."

Was that what a painting of a nude woman with the head of a horse was supposed to represent? Claudia didn't know enough about art to have an informed opinion, but it seemed … off. So did Julian. He tried too hard to be innovative, too hard to shock people.

The other guests kept up a steady stream of chatter as they tried to revive Julian's spirits, until they reached the house.

Ezra was the first to alight from the vehicle, taking Claudia's hand to help her out. His gaze met hers, a softness in his expression. Trying to reassure her, she guessed. She appreciated it.

Julian began barking orders as soon as they crossed the threshold, assigning rooms, telling his guests where they could find and change into their costumes. With a beleaguered sigh, Ezra led Claudia to their adjoined rooms.

It was quieter in their wing, something Claudia was grateful for. Casting a glance on either side of the corridor to make sure they were alone, she furtively whispered, "I think Julian summoned something on the ship. He read from a book of curses he said he found in a secondhand shop or somewhere and used some of the pages in a piece. His Latin was passable enough."

Ezra blinked as he took in her words. Finally, he pinched the bridge of his nose between two fingers and groaned. "God damn it, not again."

"You've dealt with whatever Julian's summoned before?"

"No, of course not. I meant, God damn it, one massive supernatural adventure in my life was more than enough for me. I don't want to deal with trapped spirits or necromancy or vampires ever again."

"You met Merritt's vampire friends without me?"

"No, not yet. I'm certain they're very nice aside from their habits of feeding on human blood, but ..." He sighed, and Claudia had the distinct impression that he wanted to punch a wall out of frustration. "No. No, I'm not handling this. We should go back to Liverpool tonight."

Claudia desperately wanted to agree. Before she could volunteer to pack her things, she surprised herself by saying, "What if whatever Julian summoned isn't terrible? Shouldn't we wait and see?" The voices of other guests murmured and laughed nearby as they ascended the stairs.

Ezra quickly opened the door to his room and pulled Claudia inside. Closing it behind him, he twisted the brass key in the lock. The room glowed from the lamps already lit by servants. "What would we do? Neither of us know how to handle any of these matters."

"We could send a cable to Merritt and Ivy. They would know what to do. Or we could find Merritt's family when we get back to Liverpool. His whole family are necromancers."

Ezra paused as if considering her words. "Perhaps," he said slowly. "Although I'm not sure of Merritt and Ivy's whereabouts now, so there's no point in sending a cable to them."

"And what if it's nothing? What if Julian only summoned, I don't know, a water sprite or something and it decided to take a look around London for a spell?"

"Have you ever encountered a water sprite?"

"No, but that doesn't mean they aren't real. My God, Ezra." She stared at him in disbelief. "Your stepmother is a witch, her husband is a part fae necromancer, your housemate is a resurrected ghost brought back to life by dark magic, you watched trapped souls be physically released from bottles, and you're arguing over the possibility of sprites not being real?"

"That's a good point, actually. I suppose I don't see you as a resurrected ghost, is all."

She opened her mouth, about to ask him what he did see her as. Then she thought better of it, wanting to keep the conversation on the same track. "We should just assume that every boogeyman we've ever been warned against when we were children is real."

"What did Julian say when he read from the book?"

Claudia's heart sank. She hadn't had a chance to tell him that yet. "It was a command to a dark spirit to rise."

Ezra heaved a beleaguered sigh. "Well, fuck. So, probably not a sprite, then."

"I'm certain sprites can be terrible. If there are seelie and unseelie fae courts. There have to be good and bad sprites." Claudia understood his frustration, now wanting to smack a wall herself.

"Or perhaps it wasn't a sprite at all, or it's a single incident, or a coincidence." Ezra massaged his temples.

"Should we tell him?"

"No!" Ezra nearly shouted. Claudia jumped. "No," he repeated, quieter this time. "He'll just do it again to get a rise out of us and then we could have a bigger problem on our hands. I think we should find the book he read from and see what else is in there. You can translate it."

Claudia stared at him. "That's a brilliant idea."

Was it her imagination, but did he puff up a little at her praise? "I try."

"I mean it. That's the best idea we've had so far that doesn't involve going home."

"He'll be well into his cups in about an hour, if he isn't already." Ezra paced the room a few feet. "We'll wait until the party is in full swing, then take a look about his rooms for the book. Or his studio. It's bound to be in one of those two places."

"Do you know where they are?"

"I know the house fairly well. I think we'll be able to find it." Ezra smiled, one of his rare true ones that he only bestowed on her. The same fluttery warmth she'd felt in the steam cab reappeared. "Let's get changed into whatever ridiculous attire Julian's picked out, and re-join the party."

"OH, HELL."

The epithet slipped from Claudia's lips as soon as she saw what she was expected to wear. The gauzy fabric was lined with coarse white linen. At least she wouldn't be totally exposed. Throwing the garment over her arm, she crossed the room back to the adjoining door. "If Julian's goal for this party is accuracy, he's sorely mistaken. Unless you received a stola and I was given your toga accidentally?"

Ezra's was shirtless, revealing an expanse of skin. Both of them froze.

"Sorry." She focused on a brass lamp that bounced yellow light off the dark blue walls instead of his bare skin. She hoped he didn't notice how her breath caught at the sight.

"It's fine. What's wrong?" he asked. From the corner of her eye, she saw him pick up a long white stretch of fabric off the bed that matched the one in her hand.

She picked another thing to focus on. The stars painted on the ceiling were rather pretty.

"This is a men's garment," she explained. "If I'd

known there was a costume party after the gallery, I would've brought along my stola."

"Your brown nightgown?"

She swiveled her gaze back to him and narrowed her eyes.

He smiled.

"My brown *stola*, yes."

"You've been here for all of a day and night, seen with your own eyes what Julian is capable of producing, and you still expected historical accuracy?"

She felt herself deflate a little. "I expected something a little less scandalous. This looks like a curtain."

"It probably was created from one. I don't see how it's any more scandalous than the dress you're wearing, anyway."

Claudia felt a blush creep up her neck. Her evening dress's low-cut neckline certainly hadn't escaped Julian's notice, nor that of other male gazes at the gallery. It was the color of jade, a shade Ezra said suited her. "It isn't even a proper toga. Half of it's missing," she complained.

She finally forced herself to look at him, shirtless, and hoped that he didn't notice the blush creeping up her face. He held his in his hands. "It does appear to be missing— what's it called, the undershirt?" he asked.

"Mine only has one shoulder."

Ezra tossed away his toga on the bed. "Look, you don't have to go to this party if you don't want to. We'll figure something else out. I won't insist you do anything you don't want to."

She appreciated his understanding, but still needed to figure out what exactly Julian had unleashed. "No, I'll go to the party. I'll wear the costume." She looked at the makeshift garment bunched in her hand and sighed. "We're in this together, aren't we?"

Ezra crossed the short distance between them. His voice was soft. "Claudia."

She forced herself to meet his eyes, resisting the temptation to look at his bare chest.

"I mean it. We won't go if you don't want to. I don't particularly want to attend, either."

"Wasn't this the sort of thing you two did together before?"

"Yes, but I suppose I've matured. I find this whole affair to be embarrassing, actually. I didn't think it could get any worse after last night, but it appears I was wrong. Whatever you want to do, we'll do that."

"Do you think I'm crazy for being so insistent on finding out if Julian summoned something?"

"God, no. What makes you say that?"

Claudia fidgeted with the toga. "It's a lot to think about. It feels like I've been struck by lightning twice. First for being resurrected and again for being present when a demon or something has appeared." She paused, considering her words. "Three times, I suppose. Most people aren't ghosts bound to the mortal plane for over a thousand years."

"Perhaps you should consider yourself a lightning rod, in that case."

The quip brought a smile to her face. "Possibly, although I wish I wasn't sometimes. I'll get changed into my men's attire and then we'll see what we can do with a bunch of drunken guests." She held up the toga again. "Don't go back downstairs without me. I can't face them alone."

"I wouldn't dream of it."

CHAPTER 7

"We look ridiculous," Claudia groused. Her obvious irritation aside, she still took Ezra's arm as she always did when he offered it. It had started off as a way to physically support her as she learned to walk again, then became their habit. They set off through the house to the ballroom where the party was being held.

"It'll make it easier to blend in." Ezra leaned down a little to better whisper in her ear. "Tomorrow, we'll leave. I promise."

She bit her lip, clearly torn about his loyalties between her and Julian. "I know you want to support your friend. Why don't I go home and you stay? I'm certain I can manage a flight on my own."

The very notion sent chills down Ezra's spine. "Absolutely not."

"I promise I won't try to fly out of it."

"I'm not worried about that. There's any other number of things that could go wrong. Perhaps you should master ground transport first."

"I can walk just fine. I even remember to look both ways before I cross the street now," she retorted.

Ezra considered her words for a few seconds. Claudia had picked up living in the modern era remarkably quickly. She was literate and could follow written instructions. She probably would be able to handle a short flight from London to Liverpool, but … he didn't want her to leave him. His need for her presence was greater than his fears for her safety, which was rather fucked up when he thought about it. Certainly selfish.

Before he could form a response, she sighed and said, "I suppose it's best if I stay. Julian wouldn't know what to do if whatever he unleashed comes after him."

Relief poured through him at her reply, and with it, nervousness. He didn't want to imagine harm coming to her. "Neither do we."

"But we're in a better position to explain preternatural events. I still say we should move out of Julian's house, but we should stay in London until we've figured out exactly what he's done. I don't suppose you remember Merritt and Ivy's itinerary?"

"They're moving around Spain and Portugal by now. I don't know where exactly, so I can't send them a cable to get their opinions on this."

"Damn." She sighed. "So, let's find that book."

The ballroom was almost as warm as the alleged grotto was the night before. A string quartet played unfamiliar songs in a small orchestra pit. The musicians were clad in matching dark suits that looked too formal for the occasion. Servants hired for the evening held out trays of drinks to the guests, all of whom were costumed. Ezra spotted a couple of other people wearing similar Roman garb as his and Claudia's, but he didn't recognize them.

"I wish we could've been cats," Claudia said in his ear.

She discreetly inclined her head at a couple wearing cat ears and tails, black whiskers painted on their faces. With her free hand, she adjusted her toga's single shoulder strap. More of a sash, really, pinned in place with a brass brooch, giving credence to her theory about the costume being recycled from a curtain.

Ezra spotted Julian before he could offer a reply. Their host wore a Roman-style toga as well, albeit one that showed off more skin than his or Claudia's. A ridiculous crown of twisted copper wire and twigs rested on his head. "Dear God," he muttered.

"What?" Claudia asked, standing up on her tiptoes to see better.

"Would you consider it ironic that Julian looks like a cut-price Jesus when he may have unleashed hell tonight?"

She put her hand over her mouth to stifle her giggle.

Julian caught Ezra's eye and raised his hand. "Thaddeus!" His voice boomed over the crowd.

Ezra cringed, but obediently moved forward with Claudia.

"Took you long enough," Julian said, giving them a smirk.

Ezra didn't rise to the bait. "You're on the verge of another spectacular party."

"You were scarcely at the one last night. Palfrey!" Julian shouted. "No, you can drink what's offered. I see where you're headed. Stay out of my wine cellar."

"I thought Mr. Palfrey drank all your claret last night," Claudia said.

"I thought so too, but there's still some fine port he's yet to help himself to." Julian glared daggers at Palfrey, who shrugged and turned back to chatting with the McCabe twins. Arthur and Adelaide appeared to be mid-argument, on brand for them. To a passing servant holding a tray of drinks aloft, he said, "See to it that Mr. Palfrey is thrashed within an inch of his life if he so much as sets foot outside this ballroom or his assigned room tonight."

"I beg your pardon?" the servant asked.

"Or sternly ask him to remain out of the wine cellar, whichever you find most effective." Julian waved his hand in a way that Ezra guessed was to be dismissive.

The servant moved away.

Julian looked at Claudia, taking her in as if for the first time. His eyes widened with interest. "I picked a good costume for you, didn't I? We almost match."

Claudia took a tiny, involuntary step back. "I think Ezra and I are a better match, don't you?"

Ezra's breath caught at the words, innocent as they were. Julian's gaze met his, raising a brow, and Ezra wondered what his friend had noticed. He quickly schooled his expression into what he hoped was one of bored neutrality.

"I think it's unfair that Ezra is keeping you to himself," Julian replied.

"He isn't. If anything, *I'm* keeping him to myself." As if to emphasize her point, Claudia snuggled against Ezra's side.

He quickly adjusted, wrapping his arm around her.

"I see." Julian gave them both an unreadable glance. Something else caught his attention. "Hester! You look amazing!" He shuffled away on bare feet to speak to her.

Claudia disentangled herself from Ezra as soon as Julian left. "Should we look in his rooms now?" she murmured in his ear, breath tickling his skin.

Her nearness affected him in ways it shouldn't. It took him a couple of seconds to find his voice. "If we slip away immediately, he'll notice. He isn't drunk enough yet. We'll wait an hour or so, pretend to drink, then we'll look."

She nodded. "Please don't leave me alone here."

"I wouldn't dream of it."

The servants lowered the gas lamps' light, casting shadows across the ballroom. The only spot with halfway decent light was the orchestra pit, and the musicians squinted at their sheet music. At least no one would be subjected to a gramophone tonight. Ezra looked around for somewhere to sit and sighed. Aside from a few chairs that were already occupied, there was nowhere. He and Claudia kept to the side, watching the guests and looking for any signs of whatever Julian had summoned. If he'd summoned something; there was still a possibility everything that happened on the ship was a coincidence. A slim one, but a chance nonetheless. They accepted glasses of wine from a passing servant, taking tiny sips from them as the other guests looked their way. It was over an hour before Ezra felt confident enough to sneak away. "Come with me," he murmured in Claudia's ear.

She nodded and set aside her glass.

Tucking her hand in his, he led her away from the ballroom. If anyone noticed, they'd probably assume he was taking her back to their suite for … he felt himself color. He'd woken up a couple of times in recent weeks, the hazy, heated memories of dreams featuring her slipping away as he fully came awake. His body remembered them better than he did.

The mansion's corridors were dimly lit, but he remembered where Julian's family's rooms were from previous visits. The family wing was opposite the one where he and Claudia were staying. It still bore Julian's parents' touch, with ordinary velvet-flocked paper decorating the walls, coming up in the corners from its years of service. The carpets were thinning and in need of replacement. It seemed to be the last part of the house untainted by Julian's pretension and over the top tastes.

Did Julian even use his old bedroom? Was his moving to another space the reason this part of the house didn't look ridiculous?

Ezra placed his hand on the doorknob he knew belonged to Julian once upon a time. It turned under this hand.

Claudia was close behind him.

Ezra cautiously peeked inside the darkened room. A faint odor of tobacco hung in the air, reminding Ezra of his own former habit that he still missed. Reaching for the electric sconce he knew was on the wall next to the door, Ezra tugged its chain, spilling golden light across the room. A pile of clothing had been discarded on the floor, including a shirt he remembered Julian wearing when he picked them up at the train station.

"This place is a disaster," Claudia whispered, wrinkling her nose.

Ezra took in the sight of the unacceptably messy room and had to agree. Seeing that his friend still used his old bedroom provided a measure of relief that they wouldn't have to wander through the rest of the house. "Julian's never been one for organization." The wall opposite the bed was half covered in hundreds of tiny tiles that were supposed to make up a mosaic. The carpet had been pulled up in that corner, the bare floor strewn with more tiles and bottles of adhesive. A few projects Ezra remembered Julian producing in university were arranged on a set of shelves poorly constructed from unfinished wood, including the clockwork genitalia he'd joked about at the train station. The space was punctuated with empty plates sprinkled with crumbs, making Ezra wonder why the house wasn't overrun with mice. Perhaps it was and they had just been lucky not to run into any yet. A shudder rippled through him.

Claudia noticed. "Ugh."

Ezra spotted the unmade bed and wondered how the hell Julian had managed to get this far in life with so few practical skills. The waistcoat and coat Julian wore at the gallery had been carelessly tossed among the linens. "Ah ha!" He quickly crossed the room to check the coat's pockets. All he came up with was a small box of matches and a few coins. "Damn."

"His trousers," Claudia said, joining him. She poked through the pile of clothes on the floor with her foot, until she picked up a pair of gray and aubergine-striped trousers. With a pinched expression on her face, she checked the pockets. The left one had a tiny, black leather-bound book. "Found it!" Her voice was a triumphant stage whisper. She opened it and flipped through the pages.

Ezra put his hand over it. "We should get out of here."

"Good point." She patted her sides, as if looking for pockets and came up empty. "Damn it."

Ezra had already done likewise. "I shouldn't take pockets for granted."

"They're why I prefer trousers. That, and stockings are too fussy for everyday wear."

"We can debate the merits of skirts versus trousers later, after we get out of Julian's bedroom."

"I wonder why he hasn't made it as ghastly as the rest of the house." She looked around the room with distaste.

Ezra put his hand on the small of her back, urging her to move. "I'm certain he's working on turning this room into something ridiculous." He glanced over his shoulders at the half-finished mosaic. Most of the tiles were black. As they reached the door, the very last voice Ezra wanted to hear sounded from the corridor.

"It's coming along nicely," Julian said, voice deep and loose. "I'm running low on black tiles and waiting for more to arrive. I order them from Florence and it feels like it takes forever for them to arrive."

"God damn it," Ezra whispered. He looked around the room for a place to hide.

Claudia wore an equally panicked look on her face, the black book still in her hand. Sighing, she shoved it down the front of her toga, wedging it between her corset and skin. It left a distinct book shape between her breasts, peeking a little over the neckline.

"I'm starting the red next week," Julian added, his voice much closer.

Any second, he would open the door to find Ezra and Claudia skulking around his personal space. There was nowhere to hide: the wardrobe was missing its door. There was so much stuff piled in front of the bed that they wouldn't be able to clear it away and slip underneath. Excuses ran through Ezra's mind, none of which would pass Julian's scrutiny.

The doorknob turned. "You'll see," Julian said, then laughed.

Claudia launched herself at Ezra. Arms twining around his neck, she pressed her lips to his, a motion that couldn't have caught him more off-guard if she tried.

Too shocked to reciprocate at first, his body heated, his long-suppressed attraction clawing its way out. As soon as his conscious mind realized what was happening, his arms locked around her waist, pulling her closer to him. He kissed her back, tongue demanding entrance to her mouth, eliciting a gasp from her.

"Fucking hell."

Ezra broke their kiss to look at Julian and Adelaide McCabe. Julian stared at him with a bemused expression,

Adelaide shocked. "Christ alive, I gave you two rooms," Julian said.

Claudia didn't move, probably not wanting to risk dislodging the book. "Ezra gave me a tour of the rest of the house."

"I could've done that. I believe I offered." To Ezra, he said, "I knew it. I know you and your type."

"This isn't like you to cavort in other peoples' bedrooms, Ezra," Adelaide said in surprise.

Ezra gave her what he hoped was his own incredulous expression. "I didn't expect to see you two sneaking off together."

"We're not." Adelaide rose to her full height. "Julian wanted to show me his mosaic."

"Oh, you believed me?" Julian said, then laughed at himself. He pointed at the wall of black tiles. "Over there."

Ezra thought his heart might give out if they stayed in the bedroom any longer. Whether it was from the possibility of being caught with the pilfered book, or that Claudia was still in his arms, he couldn't say. "Please accept our apologies for the imposition," he said. "We'll be taking our leave now."

"I should kick you out of my house altogether," Julian replied breezily in a way that made Ezra suspect he didn't mean it.

"If you do," Claudia began, but she quieted when Ezra gave her a look. They had been as lucky as could be expected under the circumstances. Anyone else would have thrown them out by now.

Julian waved his hand dismissively. "Get the hell out of my bedroom." He turned a wolfish grin to Adelaide.

Claudia took advantage of Julian's gaze being elsewhere. Hand between her breasts, she hurried from the room, Ezra behind her.

He didn't breathe until they were in the corridor, Julian's bedroom door closed behind them.

Claudia reached into the toga and removed the book.

On the other side of the door, Julian laughed at something Adelaide said, their interlude already forgotten, at least for now.

Ezra was certain Julian would have something to say after he had sobered in the morning.

"What did Julian mean about you having a type?" Claudia asked in a hoarse whisper.

The memory of her kiss returned, and he couldn't believe he hadn't thought about it yet. He'd idly wondered what it would be like for months. At her question, he felt himself blush. "It's nothing."

"No, it isn't."

He scrubbed a hand over his face. Embarrassment welled up in him, and with it, uncertainty at how she might receive this personal detail. "All right. I've been well known in our circle for preferring buxom brunettes. So does Julian. It's why he's been shamelessly trying to flirt with you since we arrived." He looked back at the closed door, then eyed the book in her hand. "I don't want to be in the corridor when they come out."

Claudia stared at him, but her expression was unreadable.

"Let's go back to our rooms," he suggested.

She blinked at him owlishly, but still walked alongside him through the house to the guest wing, book tightly clenched in her hands.

He wished he could tell what she was thinking. Regret threaded through him at his honesty, even though he knew her well enough to know that she would have asked about Julian's meaning until he finally answered. As they walked along the landing that overlooked the marble-floored foyer, a scream rent the air. They froze and looked over the railing as more screams and shouts joined in. Panicked guests bolted through the foyer to the front door.

Claudia hid the book in one of the potted ferns that lined the landing, then ran for the stairs.

"No!" said Ezra. He grabbed her arm, stilling her.

She turned wide eyes to him. "If everyone is getting out, shouldn't we, too?"

Her logic was sound, and yet … "What's going on?" Ezra shouted down the stairs, but no answer was forthcoming. Guests poured out the door, into the night air. He took a few cautious steps down the stairs, Claudia close behind. She grabbed his hand and he squeezed it, grateful for the contact. They were still a team, kiss and awkward admission notwithstanding. The scent of sulfur filled the air. "Oh, my God, I think the house is on fire," Ezra said. His stomach turned over.

Claudia shrieked, a broken sob escaping her.

However, there was no heat, no flames. The sulfur odor increased, and an inhuman grunt filled the air. From their perch halfway up the staircase, they saw an abnormally tall man stomp into the foyer on … were those feet or stilts? Unnaturally thin legs and cloven feet, he realized. Ezra didn't remember seeing anyone wearing such a costume. "Hello?"

The man turned around, revealing his face. Horns sprouted from his white-furred forehead, his distinctly goat-like face twisted in confusion as he stared at Claudia and Ezra. He belched, releasing another cloud of sulfur.

"Fuck!" yelped Ezra.

The man—creature, whatever it was—paid no heed of Ezra's curse. Instead, it turned back in the door's direction and strolled away into the night.

The house was silent. Ezra stared at the open door, hardly daring to believe what he had just seen.

"I think we should look at that book now," said Claudia, her voice small. "I'm not an expert, but I believe that was a demon."

CLAUDIA RARELY SPOKE of her time as a ghost. She had been friendly with Merritt Sloan while she floated through his flat. It was *not* haunting, she insisted to herself, but their conversations had been limited to how he spent his day, the cases he took on as a private detective for hire. From the time she died and found herself as an invisible apparition, she followed what felt like an innate code of conduct among the deceased: do not approach other ghosts or ask them their stories. Do not take up residence in a place that already has a spirit. Do not approach beings from other planes. She had no idea how it happened, but she'd been blessed with a sense of manners after her death. A sense of manners, and an ability to recognize other preternatural beings for what they were.

And the *thing* that had just raced through Julian's house into the night was definitely a demon.

Julian stomped through his house like a disgruntled child, all of the guests having bolted except for Claudia and Ezra.

Still clad in their ridiculous costumes, the pair of them

sat ramrod-straight on a blue velvet-upholstered chaise longue in the ballroom that had seen any amount of fornication before the party ended. Neither of them spoke as Julian ranted. In Claudia's case, she was trying to figure out how to phrase the news that he had summoned a demon. She wasn't sure what was keeping Ezra so quiet. This was the first time she had ever seen him completely silent, without a dry remark or astute observation at the tip of his tongue. Perhaps his silence was due to his shocking confession before the creature got loose. Claudia felt herself blush before she tamped down the idea. No, Ezra was too pragmatic to be thinking about such a thing when his friend might have opened a portal to hell.

"They all fucking left!" Julian roared for what felt like the dozenth time. "I don't even know who crashed the event. Did either of you recognize him?" He had asked that question before, but kept up his tirade before either could answer no. He seemed to be running out of steam.

Claudia sighed and glanced at Ezra.

Julian's brows lifted in outrage. "You do!" he shouted. He crossed the short distance to get closer to her, bending down so he could better yell at her. "What the fuck were you think–"

In half a second, Ezra was on his feet, Julian's costume bunched up in his hands where he grabbed at his neck. Through gritted teeth, he said, "Do not speak to her that way."

Claudia's breath caught as she stared at the scene unfolding before her.

Julian sputtered. "You can't–"

"I can and I will. Do not speak to Claudia that way, ever. She had nothing to do with this." Ezra shook him a little as if to illustrate his point.

Julian gulped.

Letting him go, Ezra added, "Neither did I."

Julian's expression darkened and he raised a fist. Claudia scrambled to her feet, not wanting to see them brawling like children. "I know Latin," she said abruptly.

That statement caught Julian's attention. "So what? Lots of people do."

"I speak it fluently. And if you spoke it, you would know what you said on the boat tonight. You summoned something."

Ezra gave her a look that pleaded with her to keep quiet.

Julian looked at her like she was insane. "What?" Julian said incredulously. To Ezra, he asked, "What's she going on about?"

"The book you were using for your art projects is full of curses. I know something about them." An idea struck her. "I studied them at university."

Ezra closed his eyes briefly. She made a mental note to ask him if he thought she wasn't bright enough for higher education.

If Julian was suspicious about Claudia's academic credentials, he didn't let on. "I don't understand."

"You recited a spell in Latin and it worked. You summoned something. I don't know what." At his incredulous expression, she continued. "Think about it. What else is that tall? It had horns and the face of a goat! It clearly wasn't human! Didn't you see its feet?" She was nearly shouting when she finished.

Julian and Ezra stared at her, aghast.

"I'm certain you're aware of the popularity of spiritualism," she said evenly.

"What does that have to do with anything?" snapped Julian.

"It means that there are things out there beyond

human comprehension. If the dead can communicate with us, why can't other beings cross into our plane?" A sudden, horrible feeling gripped her as she remembered the decades, the centuries, with no one to talk to when she was a ghost. Merritt Sloan had been the third person in over fifteen hundred years who had been able to speak to her, and the only one willing to actually do it. She had been dead so long she'd forgotten why she hadn't moved on to the spirit plane until she spoke to him, and even then, she hadn't discussed it. Merritt speaking to her like a friend had set her sanity to rights.

Julian shook his head, then resumed his pacing. "No."

"Listen to her." Ezra's voice was firm and stern, a tone she had never heard from him before.

Julian halted. "You can't tell me you believe her?"

Doubt flickered across Ezra's features.

Claudia knew it was because he didn't want to reveal anything about her past without her approval.

"I've experienced events over the last year that have made me question my own beliefs. Furthermore, we all saw that light when you recited that spell or whatever it was. We were all knocked about after the ship tilted. You can't possibly believe that's a coincidence when we literally watched a demon run through your house?" He held up his hands and looked around the room. "My God, we're the only people who stayed behind, and it's because we *know* there are preternatural creatures running about!"

Julian didn't answer.

Ezra's gaze fell on Claudia's and held it.

"Just the smell alone, Julian," Ezra said. "Think about that. Absolutely nothing on the face of the earth could emit that kind of stink. There isn't a performance artist in existence who could produce the kind of costume or effects we saw tonight. You raised something."

Julian was silent, lips thinned. His eyes were bloodshot. Whether it was an effect of the night's drinking, anxiety about what had happened, or both, Claudia couldn't tell. "Assuming that's what happened, how do we get rid of it?"

"I don't know. I would have to read your book and hope you didn't use the relevant pages for an art project," Claudia replied.

"See here, they aren't *projects* …"

"Don't argue with me." Claudia's voice came out uncharacteristically sharp.

Both Julian and Ezra straightened.

"You've unleashed something and I'm the only person here who may know how to send it back to wherever it came from."

Julian stared at her again, expression inscrutable. "I'll get the book," he said evenly.

Claudia fought the urge to fidget in place. "I dropped it at the top of the stairs."

"What is it—is that why you and Ezra were in my bedroom? Snooping?"

"You summoned a fucking demon!" Ezra roared. "We were trying to fix your mess! For the love of God, can you just go along with what Claudia and I are asking of you? If we had told you what you did on the boat, would you have believed us and handed over the book? If—"

"Ezra." Her voice brooked no argument.

Ezra paused his tirade and nodded.

For the first time, Claudia noticed deep shadows under his eyes. The shadows, and that his mouth was incredibly kissable, but that was *not* the thing she should be focused on right now. "Let me get the book. I haven't had a chance to look through it for obvious reasons." Before either of them could reply, she left the room, tracing her steps back to the stairs. She stepped into the foyer when a cold spring breeze had goosebumps popping up along her skin. A glance at the front door showed that it was still ajar. The view beyond the open door was pitch black, unexpected for a well-populated London neighborhood. Claudia hesitated at the foot of the stairs, unsure if she should get the book back or close the door first.

It's so dark outside!

The book it was. She lightly padded upstairs and found it on the landing. Gripping it in hand, she descended again, summoning her courage to close the door. As she placed her hand on the knob, it was blown open, as if by a gust of wind. The odor of sulfur returned. Claudia's stomach turned over and she broke out in a cold sweat. She turned around and bolted for the ballroom as a familiar, horrifying roar filled the air.

"It's back!" she screamed, not daring to look behind her.

Ezra met her before she could dash into the ballroom. He wrapped his arms around her in a bear hug as he spun her around, putting himself between them. "Fuck me," he breathed, voice vibrating against her through his chest.

Claudia wiggled away enough to get a look at the beast herself. It was just as she remembered: tall, standing upright on cloven feet, with the face of a goat. Its body was covered in gray fur that peeked out from the white sheet-like thing wrapped around it. It bore a look of ... was that confusion? Could demons be confused?

It halted and looked around the corridor with beady black eyes. Its gaze settled on Ezra and Claudia for a half a second before it looked away. It took a couple of small steps from side to side, as if it was looking for someone.

"Julian," said Claudia aloud.

"Christ almighty." Julian sounded like he was behind

them, probably watching the spectacle from the ballroom. His voice held a note of terror and disbelief.

"Send it away," Claudia urged him, not taking her eyes off the creature.

"What?" Julian's reply came out higher-pitched than he'd likely intended.

"Or tell it to get into the ballroom and leave it there." Her mind worked furiously, trying to think of a solution to their problem. It had come back; probably looking for Julian since he was the one who summoned him. "I think it could listen to you. It's worth a try."

"Are you fucking serious?"

"Yes!" she snapped.

Ezra jumped, then tightened his hold on her.

"Tell it to get in the ballroom, Julian," Ezra commanded.

"Oh, fuck. All right. Get in there," Julian ordered. Claudia craned her neck to see him better. He stood just beyond the ballroom's doorway, finger pointed inside like he was a father telling his child to go to his bedroom immediately.

The creature tilted his head to the side, as if he was actually listening. Hope flared in Claudia.

It was dashed just as quickly when it roared again. It swayed on its feet before turning around, belching a cloud of sulfur in its wake. "Wait!" Claudia cried. "Julian, try saying, '*Step in cubiculum.*'" Desperation had crept into her voice, and she struggled not to panic.

"What … ugh. *Step in cubiculum.*"

The creature paused, then turned around. With heavy, echoing steps, it lumbered past Claudia and Ezra.

Julian' finger still pointed to the room, his hand shaking with fright.

The creature walked in and stood in the middle of the

polished floor, amid a wreckage of dropped champagne glasses, bits of costumes, and broken bottles. It didn't move.

Claudia broke free of Ezra's hold and slammed the doors shut. She turned around, leaning her back against them. Triumph brought a smile to her face. "Perhaps that will keep him for a time."

"What the hell was that?" Ezra said in awe.

"I thought demons might be like summoned spirits. The same person who calls them has to put them back."

"Summoning spirits?" said Julian, as if that couldn't be possible after what he had just witnessed.

"Yes. You've ordered him in there, and he'll listen to you. He can't wreak havoc across the city, at least." Exhaustion pulled at her, but she ignored it. "Let's look at that book and see what Julian has really done."

WITH THE CREATURE safely secured in the ballroom for now, Ezra, Claudia, and Julian retreated to the grotto. The room felt disgusting thanks to that stupid water tank, but it was close enough to the ballroom that they could hear if the creature got loose.

Julian paced across the room, occasionally running a hand through his mussed hair. Claudia sat on a squishy velvet chaise that had seen better days, stockinged legs drawn up under her. Ezra took a spot next to her.

She was quiet as she leafed through the book, occasionally reciting translated spells aloud. "A lot of this reads as nonsense."

"Wouldn't spells sound nonsensical to anyone who didn't speak the language?" Ezra asked.

"I do speak the language, though." She held out the

book to him so he could see what she was talking about. "The literal translation to this says, 'Structure blue green toy,' and the next line says, 'Flight water carrion tree.' It's simply random words thrown together. There are a couple of passages that make sense, but they're garden variety curses."

Julian halted his pacing long enough to ask, "What kind?"

Claudia shrugged. "A curse for a neighbor who you think caused your cow's milk to spoil, that sort of thing. Petty revenge. They were fairly common throughout the Roman Empire."

She flipped to the beginning of the book.

Ezra leaned over to better see the title, which read simply *CURIOSITIES*. "Turn the page," he urged her.

Claudia did so.

On the other side of the title read *Curiosities—A Compilation*. There was no author listed. "Where did you get this?"

"I bought it from a secondhand bookshop off in the East End. Perhaps we should visit the shop and see if the proprietor knows anything about it," Julian replied.

Ezra felt as if searching for the author at a used bookshop would probably be futile, but it was the only thing they had to go on so far. "Let's do that in the morning," he agreed.

"Would contacting a priest be prudent?" Claudia asked.

Both of them stared at her for a few seconds. In Ezra's case, it was because he felt like an idiot for not considering that earlier. He'd only been thinking about necromancers and the power they wielded, what he knew of their terrifying abilities. "Of course," he said slowly. "Catholic or Church of England, do you think?"

Claudia looked at him blankly. "Not a clue. I'd hoped one of you could decide which would be best. I've never set foot in a church."

"How?" Julian asked.

"I'm not certain that's relevant …"

"I was baptized Anglican," Ezra said, wanting to keep their conversation on the topic of the monster waiting in the ballroom.

"Catholic," Julian admitted. "My mother insisted. Catholics believe in all sorts of things that the Anglicans have given up on."

"So, tomorrow we'll visit the nearest churches and ask the parsons about exorcisms or holy water," Ezra said.

Julian nodded.

Some of the tension line bracketing his mouth smoothed out. Ezra knew his had to be the same. "Claudia will visit the bookshop and see if the proprietor can tell us anything about it, and possibly look for another copy."

"Just in case you tore out the relevant pages for the spell," Claudia piped in.

"You wouldn't happen to have those pages, would you?" Ezra asked, already suspecting the answer.

Julian colored. "Technically yes, but they've been shredded into a fine paste and applied to a sculpture with red paint."

Frustration welled in Ezra, replacing his cautious optimism. "God damn it, why couldn't you just use a fucking newspaper? Why do you have to make a production about *everything*? No one would have known if you used newsprint for your work!"

"My apologies for not considering the possibility of summoning a demon when I create," Julian snapped.

An unexpected burst of rage flared in Ezra. He had to force himself not to leap off the chaise and grab Julian by the collar as he'd done earlier. He nearly shouted something about pretension, wanted to demand why Julian had to be so fucking obnoxious about everything. Claudia's hand on his arm silenced him. He glanced at her, saw the quiet pleading in her eyes. She didn't want to witness a full-blown brawl on the grotto floor, which would be a certainty if Ezra rose from his seat. Instead, he replied wearily, "I know. All right, the thing is contained for now and seems to listen to you. First thing tomorrow morning, we'll look for churches and the bookshop." He stood and held out his hand for Claudia. "We should get some sleep."

"You can't be serious," Julian said.

"I am."

"How can you sleep while there's a monster in the ballroom?"

"Claudia's about to fall over from exhaustion, so easily. Why don't we take shifts? If you're up for it, you guard the ballroom for a couple of hours, then come and get me and I'll take watch while you nap."

Julian nodded. "That seems reasonable. I'll make some coffee and get my sketchbook."

Ezra rolled his eyes.

"It helps me stay awake!" he insisted.

"Will you be all right to make coffee now that your servants have fled?" Ezra asked.

"I'm not completely incapable. I can boil coffee. I'll even save some for you." Some of Julian's characteristic teasing note had returned to his voice, a reminder of the friendship he and Ezra had once shared.

"What about me?" Claudia asked.

Ezra's response was immediate. "You'll sleep."

"I can help."

"No." Ezra's voice was firm. "We've established that

the demon, creature, whatever it is, will listen to Julian only. There's no need to put yourself in danger."

"It will listen to Julian if he's speaking Latin," Claudia corrected him. "If you insist on my staying put and out of the way, at least let me write down some phrases he can use if it leaves the room."

Damn it, there she was with that logic again. It was difficult to believe this was the same woman who forgot she was solid flesh and bone, who had tried to walk through walls mere months ago.

Julian left the room in search of his sketchbook, leaving Ezra and Claudia alone.

Despite the danger they had faced and the ever-present scent of sulfur in the air, awkwardness descended over Ezra. He now had time to contemplate their kiss. Unexpected heat rose in him, along with the notion that he definitely wanted to do it again. How the hell should he approach this?

Another time.

She probably remembered Julian's quip about his preference for women like her when they were at university. True as it was, the remark stung. Claudia could only feel odd about it. He certainly would, if a friend of hers casually announced that blond men always caught her attention. Perhaps he should address it, if only to apologize for Julian's blustering. He faced her, mouth dry. "Claudia." He was interrupted by Julian returning to the grotto brandishing his sketchbook and a pencil.

"The monster's still caged," he announced, his voice almost cheerful. "I pressed my ear to the door and heard some scratching, so he seems to be settling in for the night."

That was a minor relief. "We'll take our leave then," Ezra said.

Claudia nodded, nearly drooping under her exhaustion.

"It's just past two. I'll wake you at half-three," Julian said.

"That's fine." Enough for him to snatch a little sleep. "Claudia, let's go."

She nodded again and took his arm before he could offer it.

That same heat was stoked in him again at the small contact. Perhaps she wasn't bothered by Julian's earlier revelation, or she had forgotten. She didn't bother to suppress her yawn. "Good night, Julian."

CHAPTER 9

Despite it being his time to sleep, Ezra couldn't do it. He lay in bed, fingers laced behind his head. He had left a lamp turned on low, the first time he'd needed a night light since he was a boy. If something happened with the thing in the ballroom that required his help, he didn't want to waste time fumbling around in the dark in an unfamiliar room. At least Claudia was safe, locked in her room as she was. He hoped she was getting some rest. She looked ready to drop to the floor before she collapsed on her bed.

Thinking of her made him remember their kiss all over again, despite the danger waiting for him downstairs. He didn't know which was keeping him awake. He turned on his side and squeezed his eyes shut, hoping the change in position would help him get at least a few minutes of shut-eye. According to his watch that he'd left on the nightstand, he was supposed to take his shift in less than an hour. He'd just started to drift off into a light, Claudia-scented sleep when a knock at the door had him alert again. It creaked open before he could say anything.

Julian's head popped into the room. "Your turn," he said in a stage whisper.

"Damn." Ezra threw off the bedcovers and hauled himself upright, muscles creaking in protest. "I'll be right there." He quickly dressed and met Julian in front of the ballroom. The doors were still closed, with Julian sitting on the floor in front of them. The sulfur stink remained. "How has he been?"

Julian shrugged. "He's been quiet, although I can hear him shuffling about sometimes. Do you suppose he's really a he?"

"Is this what you're thinking about?"

"It's a perfectly valid question. The Biblical demons all seem to be male." Julian nodded his head at a leather-bound Bible, which Ezra hadn't noticed until now.

"I thought you were going to sketch all night."

"I did, a little." Julian picked up his sketchbook, waiting beside the Bible. He flipped through it, then held it up to show a picture of the creature. Ezra shuddered, then sat next to Julian.

"I thought I should brush up on my Bible studies before going to the church this morning. It's been a while. Do you think the priest will hear me out if I haven't confessed in, well, years?"

"If they make you confess before the priest will consider exorcising the demon, you're going to be in the booth for a few hours."

Julian sighed. "More like a couple of days."

"A month, possibly."

Julian gave a humorless laugh. "A long time."

He made no move to get up. "Are you planning on sleeping here?" Ezra asked.

"I don't think I can sleep at all. I thought I'd keep

watch with you, if you don't mind. How the hell did you get any rest?"

"I didn't. I'd just started to nod off when you called me for the shift change."

"Sorry about that." Julian actually sounded genuinely contrite.

"None needed."

"Look, I'm sorry about all of this." He gestured around the corridor, as if the creature was before them.

If this wasn't a potential matter of life or death, if their safety wasn't at stake, Ezra would have made a sarcastic remark or two about Julian's hideous, over the top home. He would have accepted his apology for inflicting his shameless, and frankly terrible, Bosch imitations on his eyes. Not to mention the fucking grotto that would end being the source of an outbreak of something terrible if its water in the tank wasn't changed or filtered. "How were you to know you were summoning something when you read from a used book?" he countered.

Julian gave a half-shrug. "I'm still responsible. Thank God for Claudia and her Latin knowledge." With that last statement, Julian gave him an unreadable look, as if he was waiting to see Ezra's reaction.

"Agreed," he replied, voice neutral.

"Hell of a thing that she knows the language and had some ideas as to how to get rid of *that*." As if on cue, stomps sounded on the other side of the doors. A shudder rippled through Ezra at the thought of the beast's cloven feet. "Necromancy, what a thing."

Ezra's disgust at the creature gave way to suspicion. It was one thing for Julian to know that preternatural creatures existed; it was another to give away Claudia's secrets. "Well, she's fairly well-versed in these matters." There. That was a noncommittal answer that gave credence to her knowledge without letting it slip she was resurrected from the dead. Literally conjured out of thin air to her physical body by dark fae magic.

"We should chat sometime, the two of us. After this unpleasantness is over, do you think she would be willing to help out with my art? She could pose for me as a succubus."

Jealousy flared to life once again, and with it, a desire to clock his friend in the face for suggesting such a thing. "Absolutely not."

"Are you going to grab me by the throat again if I ask her directly?" A mocking note had crept into Julian's voice.

It dared him to give into his baser instincts and beat the shit out of him. For summoning a demon, for making passes at Claudia, for his entire undeserved art career—all valid reasons in Ezra's eyes. He met Julian's gaze and held it. "I might."

Julian's face relaxed, a broad grin replacing his smirk. "Jesus. She really has you in knots, doesn't she?"

Ezra opened his mouth to retort that she didn't, thought better of it, and closed it. He stared straight ahead, focusing on a statue of a stone owl that he vaguely remembered from previous visits.

"If she does, I don't know why you won't do anything. You never had a problem in that regard before. What's changed?"

Everything had changed with the death of his father, then Ezra's business with necromancers, his stepmother revealing her own powers, all of the events of the previous autumn. "I'm not the same person I was the last time we saw each other."

"Since you met Claudia?"

"Yes."

"How did you meet her, anyway?"

The conversation started to tread on dangerous territory. A flash of inspiration struck him. "She's a cousin of my stepmother's new husband."

"And you've been hosting her in Liverpool ever since?"

"Mm-hm."

"I don't understand it. She's exactly your type, you're clearly attracted to her, you're living together, I think it's fairly obvious she feels the same about you, and …"

"Enough!" Ezra's response came out louder than he intended, causing Julian to startle. "Our situation is quite complex."

"Would Ivy's new husband kill you?"

"I wouldn't put it past him." That was putting things mildly. One of the last things Ezra wanted to do was piss off a man who could wield the kind of magic only found in books written solely to terrify children.

A sudden thud against the ballroom doors had them scrambling to their feet. On the other side, the creature bellowed.

"What the hell does it want?" Julian cried, grabbing his sketchbook. He opened it to the page where he'd scribbled all of Claudia's Latin phrases. "*Menere tranquillitas!*"

Silence descended on the room. Relief swept through Ezra, only to be dashed by the sounds of breaking glass.

"God damn it, it's broken through the garden doors!" Julian yelped.

Ezra had forgotten about the glass doors that led to the back garden. "Fuck!"

Julian wrenched open the ballroom doors before Ezra could offer a word of protest. They were hit in the face with the stench of sulfur. There was something else underneath it that reminded Ezra of the séance last year that brought Claudia into his life, what he imagined brimstone to smell like. What was most distressing was that the creature was gone, presumably having punched its way through the space where the glass-fronted doors used to be. He and Julian bolted to the other side of the room to assess the damage. The creature stood in the garden, looking perplexed at the flowerbeds and shrubs covered in burlap. It turned around to face Julian, as if waiting for an order.

"Stay there," Julian said. "Uh … *manere. Ibi manere?* I don't remember the words. Come back inside."

The creature looked up at the sky mournfully and wailed the way Ezra imagined a wolf might. It turned away from Julian and began to walk in the opposite direction of the house before breaking into a run.

"Damn," said Ezra.

"Let's go." Julian's voice was grim.

They took chase of the creature, dashing after it as quickly as their exhausted bodies allowed. They were no match for it as it bounded on its long legs across the property, then leapt over an iron fence on its edge as easily as a hare would. Julian leapt at the fence, then slid down to the grass, struggling to catch his breath. So was Ezra. His heart sank as the creature disappeared from sight.

"Fuck!" Julian's roared epithet was as loud as the creature's bray.

"Perhaps it'll come back. It did before."

Julian scrubbed his hands over his face. "Oh, God, it's loose. It's fucking loose again!" He groaned. "Do you think it could be shot and killed by a constable?" he asked hopefully.

"Not a clue. If it's a demon, I don't know if it can be killed."

Julian rose, leaning against the fence's iron bars. "What do we do now? Should we look for it?"

"How would we get it back to the house? It seems to listen to you selectively even when you're speaking Latin."

"I told it to stay still before it ran off," Julian replied miserably. "Perhaps my pronunciation was off."

"We'll ask Claudia about that later in the morning." A ragged sigh escaped Ezra. "Let's go back to the house and see if it returns."

The walk back to the house was silent as their ears strained to hear the creature's bellows or screams from Julian's neighbors. The ballroom came back into view, a strange orange light casting a warm glow over the garden. No, not light, Ezra noted with horror. Fire. The creature must have set it before it took off, breathing sparks on the curtains that none of them had noticed in their fright. Without another thought for his safety, Ezra shouted, "*Claudia!*" and ran the rest of the way to the house, Julian at his heels.

The curtains were already ablaze when they reached the hole where the doors used to be. Flames licked at the ceiling as sparks showered over a velvet-upholstered chaise. "Oh, my God," said Ezra, not knowing where to start. A quick glance at Julian told him that his friend was unsure, too.

"Get Claudia and get out," Julian ordered.

"What about …?"

"I'll handle it!" Julian snapped. "Just get Claudia and get the fuck out of the house!"

Ezra hesitated for half a second before he nodded and bolted from the ballroom. A glance over his shoulder revealed that the corner of the room where the doors had been was ablaze and spreading quickly.

Julian shoved him out of the way and closed the interior doors behind him.

If Ezra had thought the mad dash across the garden was torturous, the race to Claudia was monumentally worse. What if she had woken up and left the room? What if the rest of the house caught fire before he could find her? Heart in his throat, he slammed her bedroom door open, breaking its lock in the process with a pop.

"Ezra?" Her voice was sleepy.

"Get up. The house is on fire," he ordered.

A shriek escaped her, a sound he had never heard before from her. "Fire?"

"The demon did it when it escaped. There's no time to get your things, get out of bed now!"

Claudia's response was immediate. Still wearing her toga costume from the night before, she nearly threw herself into Ezra's arms. Her whole body shook with terror. A sob escaped her. "I hate smoke."

"It's all right," Ezra lied. He didn't dare let go of her hand as they dashed through the house. The scent of smoke crept into the air when they reached the foyer, overtaking the sulfur. Ezra had never smelled anything worse in his life.

Julian waited at the front door. "I've telephoned for help. They're on the way."

"You have a telephone?" Ezra couldn't help but ask.

"What's a ..." Claudia's voice trailed off as Julian nearly shoved them outside the house, slamming the door behind him as he did so.

They waited in the front garden for what felt like an interminable amount of time, until the sound of rotors above had them looking up. A giant ornithopter flapped above them, the seal of the London Fire Department glowing on its side. A smaller one trailed behind, both of them coming to undignified landings on the grass. Mounted on the afts of each craft were giant tanks, far larger than the ones required for fuel. Four men wearing bulky suits hopped out of the flying machine and unspooled a length of hose. Three of them pulled heavy helmets over their faces, while the fourth approached Julian. "This is the house, sir?"

Julian opened the door. "The ballroom. Back of the first floor, to the left of the foyer. The interior doors are closed."

The man nodded and pulled on his own helmet. The four of them burst into the house, each carrying a length of the hose. Another pair of firemen had jumped out of the smaller ornithopter. He immediately turned wheels and levers on the tank of the larger craft. It groaned and creaked for a few seconds before the hose filled with water. "More are on the way," one of the men said, a little too cheerfully for Ezra's taste. The rapid clacking of a steam vehicle's wheels against the road confirmed that statement.

A shaking Claudia snuggled against him, wrapping her arms around his chest. Ezra did likewise, needing the contact and comfort as much as she did.

CHAPTER 10

JULIAN'S HOUSE WAS SAVED, but wouldn't be habitable for quite some time. Claudia tried to follow along with the firemen's reports, gathering that the ballroom was destroyed and much of the first floor was damaged from smoke. Julian argued with them, insisting he needed to be there, but was rebuffed. Parts of the house were at risk of collapse until they could be repaired.

"Stay with me," Ezra said at last when Julian finally slumped his shoulders in defeat.

"You want me to haul myself all the way to Liverpool?"

Ezra sighed and pinched the bridge of his nose between his fingers. "No, you idiot. I have a townhome here, remember? It has enough space for all of us."

Julian looked around before he replied, voice low. "What about the … thing?"

"We could come back tonight, or it might make an appearance at my home, I don't know," Ezra said. He sounded despondent at the possibility of it appearing at his home.

"I think it's bound to you," Claudia piped up. "It did listen to you."

"It set my fucking house on fire!" Julian returned in a furious whisper.

"We'll figure that out later. We still have a bookshop and churches to visit if we hope to get rid of that creature." Ezra sniffed his clothes with disgust. "Not to mention all of us could use a good scrub. Christ, but we stink."

Claudia discreetly did the same and grimaced. She had either been too tired to care about the sulfur fragrance, or she simply didn't notice it anymore after a spell. Mixed with the smell of the fire, it made for an unfortunately potent combination.

"Do you have any employees left, or did they all flee into the night?" Ezra asked Julian.

"None of them live at the house, and everyone who served the party last night was hired from an agency. I told you, I don't keep staff like that. I have a hired driver, a couple of housekeepers, and a cook who stops by every few days," Julian replied.

It still sounded like a lot of people who kept him and his house in order. Far more than the housekeeper Ezra hired to stop by once twice per week to dust and prepare meals. When Claudia sneaked a glance at Ezra, his expression told her he had to be thinking along the same lines as her.

"Where is your driver now?" he asked.

"It's hardly dawn, so he's probably still asleep."

Ezra closed his eyes, a gesture that highlighted the deep shadows beneath him. The poor man, he'd hadn't any rest. "I will hail us a cab, and we will go to my house," he said evenly.

"Do you suppose the firemen would let us go inside and get our things?" Julian said hopefully.

"Do not bring mosaic supplies into my house."

"I won't."

"No mural painting nor papier mâché will be done in my house."

"Oh, my God. I'm going to get some clothes!"

"Ezra," murmured Claudia. "Don't bait him. His house was on fire."

Ezra looked down at her, eyes widened in surprise.

They were permitted to return for a few minutes to collect some personal belongings. Claudia's gorge rose at the hideous smell that permeated the place: sulfur, smoke, burned paper and carpet. She cast a gloomy eye around her sunny bedroom, still so cheerful despite the damage downstairs. Even if she didn't care for the rest of the house or its owner that much, she did like this room. With a weary sigh, she shoved everything she brought with her into her bags, leaving them on the floor. She slipped into her own jacket, draping Ezra's over her arm. She poked her head through the ajar door that connected her room to Ezra's. "Are you ready to leave?"

He had just finished buttoning a linen shirt, creased from its time in his luggage. His discarded toga lay on the unmade bed.

Her mind flashed back to the night before, when he was changing his clothes, how she had seen him half-dressed. How the sight set a kaleidoscope of butterflies racing through her stomach. Of course, when she thought about that, she remembered their kiss, even if it had only been for their cover. *I'm actually sad that wasn't real.*

She started. Where had that thought come from? Ezra was her friend.

He cast a glance around the room. "I think so."

Claudia held out his jacket. "You might want this. It's chilly outside."

Ezra crossed the short distance between them and took it. "Thank you." He put it on, fussing with the cuff for a few seconds, not meeting her gaze. She thought he might have something to say and was screwing up the courage to do so.

Julian bellowing down the corridor had both of them jumping. "We have to get out!"

Claudia looked behind them when they left, sighing at having to leave such lovely rooms. When she turned her gaze straight ahead, a painting of a nude man with clocks where his head and penis should be sent a shudder down her spine. Perhaps not.

They found Julian outside, speaking to the firemen about the damage, what kinds of repairs needed to be made. From what Claudia could parse together, it sounded like the ballroom and a large section of the foyer would have to be rebuilt altogether, and the airing out of the place would take weeks.

"What in God's name do you do in there?" one of them asked. "We've seen and smelled everything there is, and I've never been slapped in the face with that odor."

Julian fidgeted for a couple of seconds, like a small child about to confess to stealing sweets. "Nothing untoward. I'm an artist. I use a lot of mediums in my work."

"Yes, we gathered that." The firemen exchanged glances with one another. One of them looked like he was trying not to laugh.

Despite her frustration with Julian, sympathy flickered in her at their reactions. His art was derivative, pretentious, and tried too hard, but he clearly worked hard and was proud of it. Having a demon wreck one's first major art installation and then try to burn down the house after the fact was just salt poured in an open wound.

"Are we finished here?" Julian asked impatiently.

"We are. You're free to go."

"Free to go where?" Julian muttered.

Ezra clapped him on the back. "My townhouse, you know that. Let me hail a cab, and we'll head there now."

HIS LONDON TOWNHOUSE had been bequeathed to him by his mother. It was one of the smallest on the street, an old, narrow brick home too small to comfortably house a family with children. During Ezra's university days, it had served as a refuge for him, a place to escape from his father and Ivy during the holidays. It had never been a gathering place for his friends, and Julian had only been there a handful of times. Ezra hadn't stopped by in a couple of years.

When he unlocked the door and stepped into its foyer, he was pleased to see that the cleaning company he had hired kept up with their work. The house smelled of cleanser overlaid with bergamot fragrance. He was too tired to fully appreciate it. "Here it is," he announced wearily. "The bedrooms are upstairs. The gray and pink room is the one I use." That one had been his parents' bedroom, once upon a time, and before that, his maternal grandparents. The foyer opened to a short corridor, at the end of which was a carpeted staircase. To the left was a parlor, still decorated with a floral motif as Ezra's mother left it. To the right was a sitting room he had converted to a makeshift studio, the kitchen off of it. Upstairs were three bedrooms and a fully modernized water closet, complete with a bathtub and running water like his flat in Liverpool. He would have nothing less in his home.

Julian looked around the space, disapproval on his features, but he didn't comment on the lack of apocalyptic-themed paintings or nude statues. "Right then. I'll be taking a nap." Without another word, he headed for the stairs.

Ezra and Claudia watched him leave. "Why don't you go to bed, too?" he asked her.

"I've already had some sleep." She poked him in the chest. "*You* need to get some rest. You've been awake for days."

She didn't move her finger immediately.

Ezra felt the small touch as acutely as a brand. He reached for it, wrapping his fingers around her hand. He delicately traced the lines of her hand and wrist, as if memorizing the feel of her warm skin.

She inhaled sharply when his thumb slid over her pulse, a reminder that she was still alive.

The memory of their kiss resurfaced, and with it, the desperate need to repeat it. Part of him wanted to make sure his reaction to her wasn't a fluke, to find out if her lips were as soft as he remembered. His breath stilled as he fought to control himself.

"Ezra?" Claudia's voice was breathier than usual, but still effective.

He let her go.

"Julian's probably taken the big room at the end of the corridor. There's a smaller one next to mine, if you want to take it. It isn't sunny like the one you had at his house, but I'm certain you'll still like it." By his standards, he was babbling. Why the hell was he babbling?

Claudia raised a dark eyebrow in a silent question. She

must have noticed it, too. "All right. As long as I'm within screaming distance."

He hadn't been expecting that response. "What?" His reaction finally coaxed a smile from her, the first she'd had since the demon stomped his way through Julian's house.

"I'll take that room, and a bath first thing."

"Will you be able to manage the taps?"

She gave him a withering look. The impulse to kiss it off her face was strong, but he tamped it down.

"Are they very different from the ones in your flat?"

"No."

"Then I'll be fine." With another smile, she picked up her things and headed up the stairs.

Weariness pulled at Ezra. He yawned, a reminder that he hadn't slept in God knows how long. But being in his mother's house reminded him more than ever of his manners. With a sigh, he checked the kitchen to see what he had. There wasn't much: salt and pepper, a tin of ground coffee that was probably stale, some unfamiliar paper-wrapped toffee that was probably left behind by the housekeeping service. With another gusty sigh, he closed the bare cupboards. He would have to get some groceries. He cautiously sniffed his clothes. *Ugh.* He still smelled like a creature escaped from the depths of hell. At least it was early enough that there wouldn't be too many people about the market to offend.

The pipes above him groaned, a sign that Claudia was taking her promised bath.

He tried not to think about her soaking in the water, droplets sluicing over her skin as she scrubbed away the previous night's stink, possibly with the French-milled soap ... he shook his head ruefully. The French-milled soap waiting on a shelf next to the bathtub had been a favorite of his last paramour in London.

How embarrassing for us both.

Ezra wrote a note on a scrap of paper left on his studio's table. He crept up the stairs and left it on the pillow of the room next to his, noting with satisfaction that Claudia's bags were tossed on the floor, already open and overflowing with her things. The bedroom door at the end of the corridor was closed, confirming that Julian had likely already passed out for the morning.

I've gone to the market for food. I'll be home soon.

The words were simple, printed in block letters because Claudia still had difficulty reading his cursive. He could hear humming from the bathroom across the corridor as she soaked in the tub, an unfamiliar tune that was probably from her first life.

Ezra left the house before he could do something stupid like stay behind and listen to her further. There was a small market a few streets away, already open at this early hour. He picked up a few things to tide them all over until … when, exactly? How long would it take to capture the demon, send it back to hell, whatever they needed to do to get rid of it? He didn't want to be in London any longer than necessary.

As he was about to pay for his things, the headline on one of the morning newspapers caught his eye: SPRING-HEELED JACK BACK FROM HELL?

He nearly dropped his groceries. "Fuck," he whispered hoarsely.

"Sir?" The shop's proprietress arched an eyebrow at him at the vulgarity.

Ezra's heart thundered against his ribs so loudly he thought she might be able to hear it. "It's nothing," he said hurriedly. "My apologies, it's been a very long night." He quickly grabbed the newspaper and tossed it on top of his purchases.

She nodded, accepting his explanation without another word as she tallied up his order and bagged it. Ezra gathered up his bags, stuffing the newspaper under his arm. This was getting worse and worse.

To her surprise, Claudia managed to snatch a couple of hours' worth of sleep. The sun was high in the sky when she stirred awake, a welcome sight. After having spent so many centuries rattling around old buildings, she would never tire of sunlight. Her good mood evaporated when she recognized the room she was in: a sedate bedroom, the walls covered in flocked gray velvet paper, an empty ewer and bowl waiting on top of a dresser.

This was Ezra's other house, the one she had never been to.

She set aside her apprehension to marvel at the notion that someone could own more than one home. Was Ezra awake? With some reluctance, she crawled out of bed—very comfortable, she noted—and pulled a thick wool wrapper over her nightgown. Padding through on bare feet, she peeked into the pink and gray bedroom next to hers. It was empty, the bed still made. A quick glance at the other end of the corridor told her that Julian's bedroom door was still closed. She found Ezra in the front room filled with art supplies, sitting at a big table covered in newsprint. The curtains were drawn, sunlight filtering through the material and picking up the gold in his hair. He had changed his clothes, and as she drew closer, she could pick up the faint fragrance of the soap she found in the bathroom.

"You could get some more rest," he said by way of greeting.

"So could you."

He held up a sheet of newspaper. "No, I can't."

Claudia silently read the headline. "What's a Spring-Heeled Jack?" she asked, already dreading the answer. The demon had a distinctive bounce to its step when it moved.

"It appears to be the nickname of a creature that allegedly terrorized a few English cities over the last fifty years or so." Ezra stared at the headline in disgust. "Moreso Liverpool, apparently, but it was sighted in London, too."

"And you think the demon Julian summoned could be this Spring-Heeled Jack fellow?"

"No, I don't give a damn if it's Spring-Heeled Jack. I don't give a damn about its name at all. It's on the front fucking page of the newspaper!"

Claudia felt like an idiot. "Of course. Is this a good newspaper, though? Is it one where people can actually believe what's in it?"

"It's *The London Owl*," Ezra explained.

"Like the bird?"

"Like a tabloid that's borrowed the name of an esteemed bird to give credence to its outlandish tales."

"So, I shouldn't feel like an idiot for asking about the name 'Spring-Heeled Jack' first, if it's a story on the cover of a newspaper that prints fiction?" she asked.

Ezra pinched the bridge of his nose between two fingers, a gesture she knew he did automatically when he was tired and frustrated. "No, you should never feel like an idiot, and I'm sorry if I ever implied you are."

She shrugged. "No apologies necessary. I know I'm a difficult person to be around."

"No!" His response was more vehement than she expected.

She jumped.

"No," he repeated, voice softer. "You're not at all."

"Once I stopped flooding your house and setting things on fire." The latter had been out of curiosity, to see if she would react in terror at the sight of flames. So far, as long as the fire stayed where it should—in fireplaces, on stoves—it didn't bother it. Even experimenting with one of Ezra's cheroots hadn't scared her too much, at least until she dropped it and he had to stamp out the smoke on the carpet before it caught fire.

I still haven't told him how I died.

She shook her head, as if to clear her mind of such distractions. He had enough to fret about without her randomly telling him how she died in a fire hundreds of years ago. And fret he would. He was remarkably protective of her. Claudia vaguely remembered hating it when her father and Marcus had been that way so long ago, but it was different with Ezra. His instinct came from a place of concern for a woman over fifteen hundred years out of her own time. Her father and Marcus's sense of protection stemmed from a need for control, not safety.

"I'm not upset about any of that. I never was," Ezra said.

"You worry about me," she interpreted.

He stood, the newspaper headline forgotten. He reached for her hands.

It was something he had to have done dozens of times in their months together, but on this occasion made her heart pound and mouth go dry. Ezra never passed up an opportunity to touch her, she realized. It was nice to have that support, that connection with someone who shared the same trauma. The longing that swept through her at his touch wasn't platonic, though. She again thought back to their kiss in Julian's bedroom and how much she wanted to repeat it.

But there was no Julian to interrupt them, no subterfuge to maintain.

She had no reason to kiss the man who she considered her best friend, an honor she had never bestowed on anyone. She forced herself to meet his eyes. His heavy-lidded gaze was heated, and she was struck by the crazy notion that he might want to kiss her again, too. He gently tightened his grip on her hands in a silent question, then bent his head. Claudia closed her eyes, breath held in anticipation.

His kiss was gentle, almost hesitant, as if he was afraid of hurting her.

Claudia eagerly responded, needing him to know that she wasn't that fragile, lightly sucking on his lower lip.

The gesture drew a small gasp from him, and he let go of her hands to clasp her waist.

His touch was heated even through her wrapper and nightgown, making her wonder what it would feel like on her bare skin. She slid her hands around his shoulders, needing him to be closer to her. His hips surged against her body, proof of his need for her pressed against her belly. Long-dormant desire flooded through her, all rational thought fled. She hadn't touched anyone or been touched like this in over fifteen hundred years. When Ezra's tongue demanded entrance at her mouth, she was only too happy to receive him, a moan escaping her. To her surprise and disappointment, he pulled away. Hands still on her hips, he put some distance between their bodies.

Claudia resisted the impulse to kiss him again, waiting for him to speak. He didn't, but he looked as if was trying to scrape the words together. Unable to wait longer, she breathlessly asked, "Is something wrong?"

To her relief, he gave a tiny shake of his head. "No. I think I wanted to do that for a long time."

His admission warmed her almost as much as his kisses did. "I wanted that, too."

Ezra lightly traced his thumb over her jawline, then her lips, as if memorizing her features. Her tongue darted out to lick him, and his eyes darkened in response. "This is quite the conundrum we're in," he murmured.

Claudia's heart sank. "How? We're both adults."

"It's not that, and I think you know it."

She closed her eyes, willing away unexpected tears. She knew what he meant: the imbalance between them. The danger they were in at the moment. Merritt Sloan himself, who might finally tear Ezra limb to limb if he knew what kind of feelings he harbored for Claudia. "What does it matter?" she asked when she spoke over the lump in her throat.

His next words sounded forced. "It matters to me a great deal. You, too."

Ire flared in her. "Oh, come off it. You're speaking from a sense of misplaced honor."

Ezra pulled away from her. Her body immediately mourned the loss of contact. "I'm trying to do the right thing here, for once in my life …"

She interrupted him. "You've been doing the right thing for months. Look, Ezra, I care for you in a way I haven't for anyone else for centuries." Damn it! She hadn't meant to say that. Her feelings for him ran far deeper than anything she'd once had for Marcus. She tried to soften her tone. "What if this is the natural evolution of our friendship?" She held her breath, waiting for his reply.

Some of the sparkle returned to his eyes. "Inconvenient timing, wouldn't you say?"

"When would the timing be convenient?" She took a small step toward him and placed her hand on his chest. His heartbeat drummed steadily beneath her fingers.

"When we aren't trying to secure a demon," he replied wearily.

Claudia's heart sank and she glanced at the newspaper. "I suppose we'll have to capture that demon, then."

Shuffling feet above their heads told them that Julian was awake.

Claudia sighed. Once again, they were about to be interrupted by him. Ezra looked up at the ceiling, irritation plain across his face. "Let's find that creature."

IT HADN'T TAKEN as much convincing as Claudia expected for Ezra to leave her to her own devices at the secondhand bookshop. Perhaps it was because neither of them wanted to get into Ezra's concerns about her safety in front of Julian, or for the sake of time, or a combination of both. Despite the gravity of their situation, Claudia felt a little heady to have that much freedom. This was the kind of trip she had daydreamed about taking when Ezra mentioned it: wandering around the streets, seeing the sights. She had never expected to set foot in Londinium again. London, she reminded herself. Funny how she remembered to call the city London in Julian's presence but still referred to it by its Roman name to herself.

They had hired a steam cab to take them to an industrial-looking part of the city near the river. Claudia wrinkled her nose at the smell, reminiscent of the train station. Their dismal surroundings were tempered by the bright spring sunshine overhead and warmth creeping into the air. Claudia would have taken a deep breath of it were it not for the fragrances of smoke and grime permeating it.

She looked around at the motley collection of buildings, a mix of small shops and large factories, their brickwork stained black in places.

"Claudia, the bookshop is on Minnie Lane. It's off that square," Julian said. He thumbed in the direction of a dilapidated wooden hut built on a small stone platform.

Steam issued from a tiny chimney in the middle. Beneath it was a man wearing a heavy yellowed apron, watching over a machine loaded with … Claudia squinted. Pastries. The treats were being dispensed from the top of the machine on slow-moving rotors. A queue had formed in front of the hut, with the aproned man handing over pastries wrapped in newsprint. Her mouth watered.

"The bookshop before the pastries," Ezra murmured in her ear. He pressed a few coins in her palm, which she immediately pocketed. She bit back a smile. He knew her so well.

"Of course," she replied.

Julian noticed their exchange and rolled his eyes. "There's a Catholic church about three or four streets over, and an Anglican one east of here." He pointed in the general direction.

"St. George's. I know where it is," Ezra said.

"Let's meet back here in, shall we say, half an hour?" Julian suggested.

"Will that be enough time? You have further to go and the priest may make you say a confession before he'll help you," Ezra said.

"Christ alive, I'll be in the box for days. If it comes to that, I'll just confess to the sins with the fewest Hail Marys to recite for penance. You two return here in half an hour and I'll be along as quickly as I can."

That didn't sound correct to Claudia, but she didn't know enough about Christianity to refute Julian. She exchanged a quick glance with Ezra, whose face had an expression that matched her confusion.

Julian said his goodbye and strode away, leaving her and Ezra alone. As soon as he was out of earshot, he reached for her hands, pulling them out of her jacket pockets. "Are you certain you'll be all right?" he asked urgently.

"It's only half an hour. It's broad daylight. I'll be fine."

He traced his thumb over the back of her hand, one of his habits with her, like he was imprinting her on his memory. "I won't be long."

"Do you really think this is going to solve anything?" she dared to ask.

"I don't know. It's worth a shot. That thing is only going to get more destructive." To her surprise, he pressed a kiss to her forehead. A shiver of desire rippled through her, reminding her of the kisses they'd shared in his house. He let go of her and started to walk away.

Claudia grabbed his coat sleeve. "Wait." Taking a deep breath, she kissed him. He nearly stumbled back in surprise, but he immediately responded, arms locking around her waist. Heat roiled in her.

Just as quickly, he let her go. "We'll talk about this later," he promised, voice rough.

Claudia didn't want to talk with him, but she nodded anyway. "Stay safe at the church."

He shrugged. "I can't imagine why I wouldn't be."

She reluctantly said her goodbye, then strode through the square, eyeing the metal nameplates hammered to the surrounding buildings until she found Minnie Lane. It could scarcely be called a lane, more of a glorified alleyway. Gas lamps blazed overhead, casting dull light on the cobbles between the buildings, a waste of fuel considering the time of day.

The bookshop turned out to be a wood-sided structure

squeezed between two tall brick buildings. A hand-painted sign in the grimy window read simply SECONDHAND VOLUMES. Behind the sign was a stack of books that had fallen over in a way that didn't look intentional. The shop appeared abandoned, but to Claudia's surprise, its door opened. A bell jingled her arrival. A chandelier filled with candles glowed overhead, the tiny flames sending wax droplets down the tarnished brass. It was the first thing Claudia noticed, a sight that had anxiety unfurling inside her. It wasn't like the fires neatly contained in hearths and furnaces, or even in Ezra's cheroots. She was surrounded by all manners of paper in a wooden house. All it would take was one errant spark to set the whole place afire, and she would be trapped inside again, unable to breathe as she fell to the floor …

"Good afternoon. May I help you?"

The voice was female, warm, and oddly familiar. Claudia shook her head as if to clear away her fears and looked around for its source. Around her were shelves and shelves of books that reached the ceiling, piles of tomes stacked on the floor in towers taller than she was. She stepped around them carefully, looking for the shopkeeper. "Yes, I came here to see if you know anything about a damaged book in my possession. One of my friends purchased it here."

"I'm merely a dealer of the printed words so many have cast off for a halfpenny. I can't promise to be of any help."

Claudia threaded her way between two towering walls of books. The candlelight was dimmer here, but when she got through to the other side, she was greeted by an electric light mounted on the wall. A table was set below the light, covered in a purple cloth, and a woman sat behind it. Claudia paused as she took in the sight. It was the only space relatively clear of books and shelves, with the tiled floor visible for a few feet. But it was the woman's appearance that was so startling. She was ethereally beautiful, for one thing: long, dark curly hair swept up on top of her head, impeccably held in place with pearl combs that glowed in the electric light. Her cheekbones were high and almost sharp, reminding Claudia of the revered Roman-era marble sculptures Ezra talked about. A cream-colored dress showed off her smooth olive skin, her throat unadorned by any jewelry. Dark eyes followed Claudia as she gingerly picked her way through the mess of books, then widened in recognition. Claudia's pulse picked up speed as her mind struggled to process what she was seeing.

It couldn't be. It's impossible.

But was it? Claudia herself had been dead for over a thousand years only to be resurrected. She thought back to the night Merritt Sloan returned to his flat after his first meeting with Ivy. Merritt had known she was a witch straight away. Claudia had asked him if she was beautiful, because in her time, witches always were. The memory of the beautiful witch who read her fortune to her less than a month before she died returned, bright and clear as if it had happened yesterday. She was the same woman who sat before her now, surrounded by books.

Neither of them spoke as they stared at each other.

Somewhere in the shop, a clock ticked the seconds by. Should Claudia confront her, ask her what she had been doing for the last fifteen hundred years or so? Or was this woman merely a lookalike? Could she have been reincarnated? Claudia didn't know if that was real, but given her previous spectral existence and the confirmation that other supernatural creatures walked the earth, being reborn wasn't out of the question.

Unsure how to proceed, Claudia removed Julian's book from her jacket pocket with shaking hands. "Hello," she said, stumbling over the word. "This is the book I told you about. My friend …"

The shopkeeper tilted her head to the side, an inscrutable look on her face. "*Salve amicus vetus.*"

Hello, old friend. Claudia dropped the book at hearing the Latin greeting. It took a few seconds for her voice to work again. "You remember me," she said, unable to bring up the words in her original language.

The woman replied in English. "But of course. It isn't often I see a client return to me thousands of years after I divined her future."

"Not thousands. A thousand and a half, perhaps a little more." Claudia finally gathered enough of her wits together to pick up the book. "How?"

The woman waved her hands around the shop. "How am I here? I could ask the same of you."

"Are you a vampire?"

She snorted softly. "No. I wouldn't be able to walk in the sunshine during the day if I was one of them. What brings you to my shop?"

Claudia could hardly believe she was having this conversation. "Just this book, like I said." She approached the table and set the leather-bound tome on the purple cloth, but she no longer wanted to ask about it. All thoughts of the demon, of Ezra and Julian fled as she tried to take in the sight of someone from her past. "How are you here?"

"How are any of us here?"

Damn it, this was the kind of response Claudia would have had in a philosophical discussion with Merritt when she was still a spirit. "Please answer the question."

"How are *you* here?" the witch countered.

"I died in a fire about a month after you read my fortune. My betrothed couldn't be bothered to save me. I stayed on the mortal plane, followed him to present day Liverpool, where I haunted the site of his house after he married another woman, and never left. I was returned to flesh and blood from dark magic last year." Over the last few months, Claudia had thought about how she would tell Ezra how she died, why she haunted Merritt's building for as long as she did. She thought her explanation would be long, filled with spots where she would have to backtrack to explain gaps in her story. She was surprised at her brevity. Perhaps it was because she didn't care for the witch as she did Ezra. There was no need to worry about insulating her feelings and reactions.

The witch lifted a dark brow in mild surprise. "What kind of dark magic?"

"Unseelie fae. The practitioner who resurrected me is dead now."

"So, there is no risk of you being returned to the earth before you live out a normal span of years."

"Or I'm killed again." The words slipped out before Claudia could contain them.

"I don't think that will happen."

Claudia gawked at her. "Do you remember what you told me in your tent? When I had my fortune read?"

"Yes. I haven't been blessed to remember everything about myself, but I recall every fortune I've ever told. You were destined to live longer than anyone else you knew."

"I died a month after you read mine!" Her voice had risen in fury and grief for her dead former self. She thought about the chandelier's candles at the shop's front door, how the small space was little more than a tinderbox. Gods above and below, she could die in a fire all over again if one of the candles slipped sideways in its tiny holder.

The bookshop suddenly felt too close. Claudia had to fight with herself to remember how to breathe.

"And then you stayed on this plane only to be resurrected," the witch replied, unperturbed by Claudia's outburst.

"Did you know that would happen?"

"No. I foresaw great tragedy in your life, but I was not privy to specifics." She rose, long cream skirt puddling at her feet. She looked like a statue from the temple where Claudia's family once worshipped. "I no longer offer fortunes for coin. The fates have chosen not to bless me with the ability to interpret futures, and I fear that business has caused a great deal of pain to my customers."

"Who are you and why are you still alive?" Was the witch like her?

"I'm a granddaughter of Apollo. I received his gift for prophecy, but the human heritage of my mother has tainted it."

Of all the possibilities Claudia thought of, the witch being descended from a god hadn't been one of them. It was a relief to find out that she wasn't a vampire or unseelie fae but an immortal of the gods. "I think that actually makes sense. What are you called?"

The witch smiled, revealing flawless teeth. "I call myself Matilda now. I've had many names over the centuries, not all of which I remember."

How difficult it must be for an immortal to remember so many details about false identities while losing the parts of their true selves. "I'm sorry. That sounds dreadful."

Matilda bestowed a smile on Claudia. "I've learned to live with it."

Claudia relaxed a little. Then she straightened, remembering that she was still in the presence of a demigod. "Can you still help me?"

"Is this about your book?"

"Yes. Someone I know used it to summon a demon last night. It was in the newspaper, or the tabloids at least."

Matilda picked up the book and leafed through it. "This has been defaced," she said with disdain.

Claudia cringed. "He's an artist and used some of the pages in a piece. They've been destroyed."

Matilda set down the book. "No matter. I'm certain I can find a spell to reverse the damage."

Claudia's heart leapt. "That would be wonderful! How?"

The witch looked over the books towering in piles and huddled on shelves. Claudia had the distinct impression that she knew what she was looking for, as if the bookshop was nothing more than her kitchen, and she was after an errant spoon. "Does your artist friend have any magical abilities?"

"None that I know of."

"The moon was waxing last night. That must have something to do with the summoning. Can you describe this demon?"

"He was over eight feet tall, with horns and cloven feet. He breathed fire and sulfur," Claudia replied excitedly. "It burned down part of my friend's house last night. Julian could control him until the morning and it listened to him until then."

"Interesting." Matilda picked up a couple of books, glanced at their covers, and tossed them to the tiled floor. "Am I correct in assuming your friend speaks Latin or Greek?"

"Neither. I had to write down some commands for him to try out on it. We guessed early on that the demon didn't understand English."

"You mean, *you* guessed that."

"I—well, yes. Can I help you?"

"No, but thank you for the offer." Matilda stood up on tiptoes to survey the books overflowing the corner of the shop. She barreled through him, pushing tomes aside until she plucked a random one from a toppled pile. "Here it is." She blew on the cover, dislodging dust. "Does your friend know what you are?"

"Julian doesn't." Julian wasn't her friend, either, but she refrained from pointing that out.

"But you have a friend who does." Matilda reached into a pocket of her dress, removing a flameless candle. She switched it on and held it over the book, leafing through it with her thumb.

Claudia's heart gave a happy squeeze at the thought of Ezra. "Yes."

"It's good to have someone in your life who knows everything about you, good and bad." Matilda stepped over a pile of books, revealing a pair of cream-colored satin shoes with jeweled buckles. If this were any other circumstance, Claudia immediately would have coveted them.

Even though Matilda said she didn't read fortunes anymore, Claudia couldn't help but ask, "Is that all I am to him?"

Matilda looked up, her expression serious. "No. His feelings for you transcend mere friendship, as yours do for him." Her tone sharpened. "Do not ask me anything else about him. I cannot risk another misinterpretation. I have to live with myself when I make a mistake. Immortality is a long time to live with errors on your conscience."

"Understood," Claudia replied in a small voice.

"Thank you." Matilda visibly relaxed. "How exactly did your friend summon the demon? Don't leave out any details."

Claudia told her of the art exhibit on the boat, how

Julian had spoken of stopping by the bookshop and buying the strange little book. How he'd recited a few lines from one of the spells, how light flashed by the boat and rocked it from side to side. Of the newspaper headlines speaking of a creature called Spring-Heeled Jack. Throughout the story, Matilda nodded and occasionally murmured unintelligible responses, the sort people used to show they were still listening. Matilda didn't speak until Claudia finished the end of her tale, speaking of the fire in the ballroom.

"I believe what has happened can only be called a cosmic coincidence," the witch said

"Can it be fixed?"

"Of course. Not with this, though." Matilda waved a dismissive hand over the black leather-bound book. "It appears that your artist friend happened to speak a command in a language this particular demon understands at a time he was close enough to the surface of the earth to respond."

"What does the waxing moon have to do with it?"

"My dear, the moon always works into these matters. Had it been full instead of waxing, your friend might well have summoned Orcus himself."

A shudder rippled through Claudia.

"Or another demon. There are more than either of us know. A cloven-hoofed demon who breathes fire and enters the mortal plane via water sounds like a bastard offspring from Mendacius's lineage to me, albeit a very stupid one if it does whatever your friend commands."

"It did run away," Claudia reminded her.

"And it will likely return tonight. Mendacius's children aren't known to be especially bright and they fear the sun. The demon probably wants to return to the underworld as soon as possible."

Claudia let herself feel hopeful. "Can we do that?"

"If there was a priest of our faith walking among us, I would say yes."

Just as quickly, Claudia's heart sank. "Ezra and Julian are speaking to the leaders in their faiths."

A line furrowed between Matilda's brows. "I doubt Christian leaders can send a demon back to the underworld. Perhaps they can force it into a vessel at best."

Claudia stilled at the mention of vessels. Her soul had been trapped in one for a few horrifying hours before she was resurrected. "No, we can't do that."

"Of course not. There's no time to find one large enough and it shouldn't be on the mortal plane anyway. The kindest thing to do is have your friend who summoned him send him back as soon as possible. The spell will only be effective once per night. It's preferable to do it over the same body of water he came from."

That would be a nightmare. The Thames was never quiet. "Oh. I don't think that will be possible."

"Then you will have to try elsewhere and hope the spell can be cast successfully. The demon may be hiding for the next night or two out of fear, or it could be looking for your friend for further instructions. I cannot say for certain." Matilda shuffled through the piles of stuff on her table until she found a sheet of foolscap and pencil. She wrote a few things down on the paper, then folded it and stuck it inside the book she'd been searching for. "This is a book about demonology and how it relates to our ... our people, I suppose. It was compiled by mortals and there are some minor inaccuracies, but nothing that would affect the spellwork needed to return the demon to the underworld." She pushed the book across the table to Claudia, who picked it up.

Remembering her manners, Claudia reached into her pocket for the money Ezra gave her. "What do I owe you?"

"This is a gift from one woman out of her time to another."

Of all the times Claudia remembered how currency worked, of course this would be the one where she didn't have to pay anything. "Are you certain?"

"Yes."

"Why are you here?" she couldn't help but ask.

"Why am I running an unprofitable secondhand book-shop? I've been alive for a long time and it can get boring. It's something to do. I speak to plenty of interesting people."

"You met Julian when he bought this book."

"I did. I remember him now. Rather pompous and thought too highly of himself." Matilda smiled at Claudia.

"Why did you sell it to him?"

She shrugged. "I thought it a harmless antiquity. He doesn't possess a shred of preternatural inclination. I didn't know he would summon a demon. My abilities didn't show me that."

"May we come back if we have more questions?" Claudia asked.

"You can go wherever you wish. I cannot promise I will have the answers you seek."

"I mean, will you still be here if I want to return in a day or two, or will you vanish?"

"I will stay here until people start noticing that I don't age. Then I will move to another part of England and start my life over again with a new name. I don't anticipate doing that any time soon. I've been Matilda for only six years now."

"Who were you when I lived in Londinium?" Claudia couldn't help but ask. She hoped it wasn't a rude question.

Matilda's voice dropped to a whisper, as if she was afraid of someone overhearing. "Aurelia. It's the one I was given at birth. But I am not that woman anymore and never will be again."

"Thank you." Claudia clutched the book to her chest.

"For what? Telling you my name?"

"For everything. You've solved everything for me."

"Except Ezra."

"You said you couldn't offer predictions or fortunes," Claudia pointed out.

"I *won't* offer predictions or fortunes. I *can* tell you that you and Ezra aren't listening to your hearts. You should."

Claudia remembered how Ezra tasted and her knees weakened a little. "I know. It's difficult to get him to see that."

Matilda regarded her thoughtfully under her fringes of dark lashes. "I can't say anything else. Best of luck to you and this demon problem."

CHAPTER 12

Wɪᴛʜ ᴀ ʙᴏᴛᴛʟᴇ of holy water in his trouser pocket, Ezra
tried not to stomp back to the meeting place like a child,
much as he wanted to. Gritting his teeth, he hoped that
Claudia and Julian would have had better luck in their
quest for help.

He spotted Claudia at the pastry tent and held back for
a few seconds, watching her as she purchased a treat. Her
long dark hair was pulled back in a braid that trailed down
her back, a few curly strands escaping. While her jacket
was a bit too big, her brown flight trousers were a perfect
fit, hugging her generous hips and arse that had caught the
attention of a couple of passersby to Claudia's oblivion.
One of them spoke to her, a leer on his face, although Ezra
couldn't hear what he said. A sense of protectiveness
swelled in him, and he quickly made his way to Claudia.
Glowering at the interloper without a word, the man
muttered something unintelligible and shuffled away.

Claudia swallowed her mouthful of dessert. "Did you
have to look at him like you're the devil?"

"Probably not."

She shrugged. "It's just as well. I think he was trying to proposition me. Here, I bought you a tart." She held out her free hand, where a newspaper-wrapped bundle waited.

Come to think of it, Ezra could use some food. "Thank you. Did you learn anything at the bookshop?"

"Gods above and below, you have no idea!" Her face lit up in excitement, and she pointed to a bench on the edge of the square. "You should take a seat while I tell you. You'd never believe me otherwise."

Cautious optimism filled Ezra. "You do realize that I'm aware of the existence of vampires, fae, and witches?"

"And a dead girl brought back to life. Yes, I get that. And we can add an immortal half-human granddaughter of a god. Anyway …"

Ezra's breath caught. "What? You can't just continue on after saying that!"

Claudia rolled her eyes. "I was getting to that part. It turns out the lady who owns the bookshop was the witch who read my fortune shortly before I died. Isn't that an incredible coincidence? She remembered me, too!"

"I think I should sit down for a minute." Ezra nodded in the direction of a bench on the edge of the square. Neither of them spoke until they sat.

"I can see how that would be a lot to take in, learning about immortals and all," Claudia said.

"I suppose it shouldn't be, considering everything I've seen over the last six months."

"It does make our situation easier. She told me exactly how to get rid of the demon." Claudia pulled a sheet of folded foolscap from her jacket pocket and handed it to Ezra. Written in a tidy script were Latin phrases.

Julian came into view, shoulders slumped.

Ezra wondered how bad his trip to the Catholic church

had to have been. "Did you get Julian a croissant? He looks like he might need one," he whispered to Claudia.

"I think he looks like he could use a drink, actually."

"That, too. Does that tent sell whiskey?"

Julian approached them, unusually morose. "Father Donovan didn't believe me," he said by way of greeting.

"What else happened? Didn't he read the newspaper this morning?" Claudia asked.

"He's a priest. He was probably reading a Bible or the *Book of Common Prayer* or some such thing."

"I doubt he was reading the latter. Some Catholic you are," muttered Ezra. Louder, he said, "I doubt priests have the time to read the tabloids."

"That paper didn't even mention my gallery opening!" Evidently, Julian was still upset that the *London Owl* hadn't found it necessary to send an art critic to the exhibit on opening night.

"Do you expect to read art reviews in the penny dreadfuls?" Ezra asked.

"If the work is good, then yes." Julian plunked down on the bench, squishing himself between Ezra and its wrought-iron armrest.

Secretly, Ezra was pleased that he'd had the foresight to block Julian from sitting next to Claudia. "I tried to tell the priest that I accidentally summoned a demon, and he thought I was mad. I asked him how much he charged for an exorcism and he said that would have to be approved by the Vatican. Utterly ridiculous!"

"Is it?" Ezra asked, a touch of sarcasm in his voice.

Julian turned enraged eyes to Ezra. His reply came out in a low growl. "Are you Catholic, Thaddeus? Do you understand the pomp and ritual?"

Ezra fought the urge to sigh. "Yes, I do. The king only wanted a divorce, after all." Claudia gave Ezra a questioning look, as if silently asking which king. "Henry the Eighth," he murmured in her ear.

"It was more than that and you know it. Anyway, Father Donovan refused to help me unless it was to take me to visit a doctor. He gave me a bottle of holy water. Somehow, I think the demon won't be amenable to me using it," grumbled Julian.

Ezra nearly pointed out that it wouldn't hurt to hang on to the holy water in case he ever came across a hungry vampire, but refrained from doing so.

"My trip to the bookshop was successful," Claudia announced.

That got Julian's attention. He straightened, the angry lines on his forehead smoothing away. "How so? Did you get another copy of the book?"

"No, but it turns out that the shopkeeper is, well ..." Claudia gave Ezra a panicked look, as if realizing she hadn't concocted a story about the apparent immortal running an obscure bookshop in the middle of London. "She has an interest in demonology and has heard of this sort of thing before. She gave me instructions for you to use to bring the demon back to you and order it back to the underworld." She patted her pocket, where the sheet of foolscap rested.

Julian stared at her in shock. A few seconds later, his face broke into a grin. "Are you fucking serious?" he yelped.

Claudia nodded.

"I could kiss you!"

"That won't be necessary," she quickly replied.

An odd sense of relief trickled through Ezra at her words. Their earlier conversation—his promises to be responsible for her—ran through his mind, twisted with regret. She had every right to kiss whoever she wanted to, yet the thought of it made something inside him twinge with jealousy. It was an unfamiliar feeling, and he hated it.

"I should kiss the shopkeeper," Julian mused.

"No, you shouldn't," Ezra said. "If anything, we should go back to my house, wait for nightfall, and you can try summoning that creature again to send it back to hell."

"The underworld," Claudia corrected him.

"Aren't they the same thing?"

"Hell is a distinctly Christian concept, so no."

Julian nudged Ezra, a grin on his face. "I really do like her."

"Not now, Julian."

Julian leaned over to better see Claudia. "He likes you, too."

"I know." And to Ezra's pleasant surprise, she squeezed his hand.

CLAUDIA WAS certain the back garden had to be beautiful when it was in bloom, but she couldn't think about its appearance now, not with a flameless lantern held in her shaking hand. Nervousness twisted in her stomach. When she glanced at Ezra, who held a matching lantern, he gave her a weak smile, a sure sign that he was just as nervous about what Julian was about to attempt.

Julian had spent the afternoon puzzling over Matilda's spells, sounding out the unfamiliar words with Claudia's help in anxious murmurs. He had fortified himself with a glass of whiskey before they set out in the garden; as he recited the spell, Claudia could detect a loose note in his voice that told her the whiskey was working. The gods knew she had heard him speak in various states of inebriation during their short acquaintance. His Latin didn't sound too bad, she mused. Certainly not fluent. If he was ever inclined to properly study the language, perhaps…

A roar filled the air, followed by the all-too-familiar scent of sulfur. Claudia stiffened and moved closer to Ezra, fighting the urge to scream and run back into the house. While nothing Matilda said or wrote in her notes indicated that the beast would be aggressive toward any bystanders during the spell, or aggressive at all despite the fire-breathing, they were still sharing space with a demon well out of its element. Unlike last night, the demon drew more attention this time. They could see it bouncing on its cloven feet, crashing through the neighbors' back gardens and over fences. "The hell is that?" someone bellowed from another garden.

"Fuck me, this was a bad idea," muttered Ezra.

"We should have gone back to Julian's house," said Claudia softly.

If Julian was paying attention to them, he didn't give any indication of it. "*Mando tibi ut redeas unde venisti!*" he shouted.

The demon jumped over the wrought iron fence separating Ezra's property from his neighbor's, landing with a heavy thump on the grass. His ears perked up at hearing Julian's words ordering him back to the underworld, beady red eyes fixing on his face. The demon grunted in response, perhaps an acknowledgement none of them could decipher.

Julian repeated the phrase: *I order you to return from where you came.*

The demon looked around the garden and shrugged his massive shoulders. Next door, a man yelled, "Someone get the constables!"

Ezra heaved a dramatic sigh. "I will *never* hear the end of this."

"Mr. Thaddeus? Is that you? What the hell do you have in your garden?"

Sighing again, Ezra called out, "My apologies, Mr. Pelham. This is supposed to be for art."

"Why isn't this working, Claudia?" said Julian, oblivious to their exchange. Panic had crept into his voice, tempered only by the knowledge that the neighbors were listening.

She hated the tremble in her voice. "I don't know. Perhaps you can try again?" How did one discreetly announce that a spell should be repeated when there was an audience of ordinary people?

"Fuck!" yelped Julian. To the demon, he said, "Could you stay there for a moment while we figure out what to do?"

The creature tilted his head, as if he was listening, then reared back to release an anguished, fiery cry into the sky. Screams sounded from the garden next door. At least he hadn't set anything ablaze this time.

Before Claudia could translate Julian's question, the demon bounded toward them. Julian darted out of his way, and Ezra grabbed Claudia, pulling her out of the creature's path. Once it had passed, the three of them followed it, Julian calling after it in broken Latin as it stomped away, down the street, its strides turning into a gallop. Lights were switched on as he bounded away from the house. From a distance, the distinct whoosh of a low-flying ornithopter's blades slicing through the air sounded and grew closer.

"God damn it," said Ezra, just as Julian exclaimed, "Fuck! The fire brigade is on the way!"

"Shouldn't we follow the demon?" Claudia asked.

"How? It's moving far too quickly," said Ezra tiredly.

"We'll have to try again," said Julian. His despair was

palpable. "Oh, God, we have to make up another story for the fire brigade, won't we?"

Ezra's reply was immediate, his idea echoing Claudia's earlier thoughts. "Performance art gone wrong."

Julian's brow raised in approval. "Do you think that would work?"

"Coming from you? Yes."

If Julian found any part of the reply insulting, he didn't let on. Perhaps he was incapable of being insulted. "All right. Let's summon the creature again. Hopefully, it'll work this time."

The rotors and siren of the approaching firefighting ornithopter stilled the conversation before Claudia could remind them about Matilda's warning, that the spell could only by cast once per night. There was no way they would be able to try summoning the beast again without having more explanations and excuses at the ready. Lies, Claudia mentally corrected herself. They were lying to everyone. There was no way to obfuscate their involvement. Ezra's neighbors knew him, and had seen the demon run to and away from his property.

The firemen who showed up were the same ones who put out the blaze at Julian's house, and were clearly irritated at having to see them again. At least they believed the performance art excuse and were pleased to see that nothing was actually on fire this time. They left half an hour after they arrived, after extracting promises from all of them to stop playing with matches.

It wasn't until they were back inside that Julian said, "Are we certain that we shouldn't try summoning the demon again? What if we went back to my house?" He looked around the kitchen as if he expected his house to magically appear.

"The spell can only be cast once each evening,"

Claudia reminded him. "And I think we'll have to complete it as the shopkeeper said we should, at the Thames."

"We should have done that in the first place," Ezra grumbled.

Claudia was inclined to agree.

"From now on, we should do everything exactly as Matilda instructed," she said firmly.

Julian actually nodded in agreement with her, thank all the gods. "We've wasted a night," he announced dully. With a dramatic sigh, he added, "I'm going to get drunk and fall asleep. Will anyone be joining me?"

"In drink or sleep? No, thank you," Claudia replied.

Ezra gave a strange cough and covered his mouth, but not before she spotted him trying to hide a smile.

What else had Matilda said? That they were ignoring their hearts. That they were meant to be more than friends. She wished like hell she could get him to see that.

"Are you amenable to my helping myself to the contents of your liquor cabinet?" Julian asked.

"If I said no, you would help yourself anyway."

Julian opened his mouth as if to agree, then closed it, thinking about his answer. "You know, I'm not so sure I would after everything that's happened. You two have been absolute saints throughout this."

Ezra's eyes widened slightly in surprise. "Thank you, I suppose. There isn't much here. The liquor cabinet in my studio should have a half-bottle of whiskey and unopened bottles of vermouth and Beaujolais. That's it. Don't drink all my whiskey."

"I'll give the Beaujolais a good home."

"Are you certain you don't want the vermouth? I would like to get rid of it."

"A remnant from Paulina? Ugh. Thank you for the offer of wine, though."

Who was Paulina? Claudia sent a questioning look Ezra's way. He colored and looked away. *Oh.*

Julian retrieved the wine, then bade them goodnight before he trudged up the stairs. Ezra didn't speak until Julian was well out of earshot. "Paulina was my ... lady friend for a couple of years," he said stiffly.

"There's no need to explain." As long as they weren't still involved. Claudia wasn't sure her heart could take that kind of news.

"It didn't end well. She wanted to get married and start a family, I ..."

"Ezra, it's all right. You were in a different place in your life. I understand that."

His pinched expression relaxed, as if he had been afraid she would be angry that he'd had other lovers. Of course she wouldn't be. She had them, too. Well, one. And he was the cause of her death. A love affair ending because each person wanted something different was hardly something to fuss over.

"You're not upset?" he asked.

"Why would I be?" She nearly blurted out that her former paramour's actions indirectly killed her, something far worse than leaving vermouth behind, but stopped herself. This wasn't the best time to bring that up, if there ever was a good time. She wished she could tell what he was thinking.

He regarded her thoughtfully for a few seconds. "I'm not the same person I was before we met," he finally said.

"You've told me that a few times. We're both figuring out who we are now, aren't we? Together?" She held her breath, waiting for his response. Matilda's words echoed in her mind.

He was quiet again, forming his answer. "Yes."

Well, that was a bit of a disappointment.

"I'm still learning to be a better person," he continued.

And to him, being a better person meant he thought he couldn't act on his feelings for her. "I know."

"Come here." He held out his arms.

Claudia was only too grateful to let him hug her.

He seemed to need the contact as much as she did.

He pressed a chaste kiss to the top of her head that she felt all the way to her toes. He smelled good, like the soap he kept at the side of the bathtub in her Liverpool flat, woodsy and masculine without a trace of the demon's sulfur. A shiver rippled through her that she didn't try to hide.

"Let's get some rest," he murmured into her hair.

Despite everything that had happened over the last few days, and her lack of sleep the night before, Claudia wasn't tired. She nodded anyway, and let him lead her up the stairs to their bedrooms.

CHAPTER 13

SLEEP WAS ELUSIVE. Whether it was because he wasn't tired or he had too much to think about, Ezra couldn't say. Perhaps it was the faint sound of Julian's drunken snores that drifted down the corridor that was contributing to his insomnia. He squeezed his eyes shut and tugged a pillow over his face. It was the woman in the room next door. Keeping him in knots, as Julian said. That was putting it mildly. Ezra was head over heels for her, had been for a long time. Maybe as soon as she tumbled to the floor in front of him during that disastrous séance all those months ago. Claudia had seeped into his life, his heart, like water to a fern's soil that had been deprived for so long.

This was ridiculous. *He* was being ridiculous.

He got out of bed and threw on an old silk dressing gown hanging from a hook on the back of the bedroom door. Before he could talk himself out of it, he padded out of the room and gently knocked on Claudia's door. He heard a rustle of fabric, a sign that she was still awake. He knew her well enough to know that she usually slept like the dead. He cringed. That was a bad simile.

She opened the door a crack. "Ezra?" she whispered, then opened it all the way. The lamp on the nightstand was turned on, casting yellow light across the room. Her bed was unmade, the book she had received at the shop waiting in the covers.

He relaxed a little when he saw the confirmation that he hadn't woken her. His relief was short-lived as he took in the sight of her. He had seen her in her nightclothes before, but this was different. She wore a linen shift that stopped above her knees, the fabric thin enough that he could see the outline of her body through it, her curves highlighted in the lamp's glow. If he looked closely, he could see the outlines of dark-tipped nipples, the shadowy vee between her legs. His body immediately responded. He ran a hand over his face. Maybe this was a mistake.

Claudia sounded curious and confused. "Ezra? Is something wrong?"

Ezra slid an arm around her waist, brought her to him, and kissed her.

A tiny mewl of surprise escaped her, but she quickly recovered and kissed him back.

Her arms slid around his neck, drawing him closer, the feel of her body through the thin shift already driving him mad. The small, logical part of his brain reminded him that this was a bad idea, that she was his responsibility and his friend. He stilled.

Claudia pulled away. "What's wrong?"

Nothing. Everything. She was a woman hundreds of years out of her time and they were in the middle of trying to wrangle a demon on the loose. Not to mention fucking *Julian* was at the other end of the corridor. "I'm not sure," he finally admitted.

"Is it me?" Her question was pained, self-conscious, and he hated that he might have made her feel that way.

"No!" His answer came out harsher than he intended. Her eyes widened. "No," he replied, more quietly. "You're beautiful. You're perfect. And I …"

"What?" she pressed.

What was the best way to phrase how he felt? "I don't want to spoil you."

She took a half-step back. "What do you mean?"

"I wreck things. I don't do it deliberately, but it still happens. My relationships with my parents, with Ivy, with my friends. What we have is rare. I don't want to wreck that, too."

Claudia stared at him for a few heart-stopping seconds.

He fought the urge to fidget in place.

"What a silly thing to say," she finally said. She reached for him, lightly stroking his cheek.

He leaned into her touch, needing more.

"What if this is meant to be—that I stayed on this plane all these years waiting for you? What if this is the natural course of our friendship? Why fight it?"

Not for the first time, Ezra remembered that she had never told him why she haunted the living for so many years. She had never told him how she died. Did it matter? Did she even remember why she had done that in the first place?

She had a point about this possibly being the natural evolution of their friendship. "All right," he whispered.

"All right, what?"

He kissed her again, tongue demanding entrance that she was only too happy to give. She reached for his shoulders, pushing away the fabric of his dressing gown to touch his skin. Breath stuttering at the contact, he had to resist the impulse to urge her to her bed.

Claudia pulled away enough to say in surprise, "You're not wearing night clothes!"

It took a few seconds for her words to register. That was the last thing he'd been expecting to hear. "I'm sorry?"

"You're not wearing any night clothes. I thought you did at home?"

"When did you ..." The memory quickly returned. It would have been Claudia's second or third night in his flat. She'd had a nightmare about being trapped in a bottle and came tapping at his bedroom door to ask if she could stay with him until her panic ended. He'd quickly thrown on a set of pajamas that had been gifted to him by his parents God knew how many years ago. "Oh, no, it was just that one time."

"Oh." To his body's disappointment, she moved her hands away from his bare skin. She regarded him under dark sweeps of lashes, eyes hooded with desire. She reached for his hands, twining her fingers around his. It was a surprisingly chaste gesture. Her voice dropped to a conspiratorial whisper, as if she was afraid someone would hear. "I should tell you first that I haven't been intimate with anyone in over a thousand years. I'm a little rusty."

Ezra barely held in a snort. Claudia looked like she was trying not to laugh. "I promise I'll be as gentle as you want me to be."

She responded by kissing him again, then pulling him toward her bed. She stopped when her legs met the mattress, swaying in place a little as if she'd forgotten it was there. To his surprise, she took a seat on the edge, not letting go of his hands. Ezra waited for her to continue, but she didn't, instead she held on to him. Even though every cell in his body had heated to a near-intolerable pitch, concern threaded through him. He sat next to her. "Is everything all right?"

Claudia nodded. "Yes. It's just ..." She trailed off.

"It's been a long time for me, too."

"Not fifteen hundred years. I'm sure I'll remember what to do," she replied wryly. Her tone and expression sobered, the sight of which shifted Ezra's concern into alarm. "What brought this on?" she asked. "You were so determined to keep me away."

Relief, faint but palpable, trickled through him. "I told you it's because I wreck relationships. I'm not good at opening up to people."

Claudia didn't try to hide the sarcasm in her voice. "I'd hardly noticed."

"I've always been this way. It's just easier."

"Except for me," she deduced.

"Except for you. I suppose sitting through the séance from hell will bring two people together in a way that nothing else can."

"Terrible things happening to two people will either do that, or force them apart." A shadow crossed her face, and he briefly wondered what had happened to her in her previous life. Just as quickly, it was gone. "Kiss me."

Ezra was only too happy to oblige. His lips met hers again, the feel of her against him electrifying. She surprised him when she grabbed a fistful of his dressing gown and urged him further on the bed until his head met the pillows. She lay next to him, propping herself up on one arm with the other draped across his chest. "What happens after this?" she asked.

He hadn't been expecting that question. His body protested at the lack of contact. "What do you mean?"

Claudia bit her lip, an alluring gesture. "Before we do anything else—what are we? This will change everything."

She was right, God damn it. As much as his body screamed at him to kiss her again, lift her thin shift to expose the delicious body he knew she had, he paused. "I thought we would keep moving forward together as we were before, but we'd also be having sex in the evenings." He held his breath, waiting for her response.

She was silent for what felt like an eternity before she burst into giggles, burying her face in his shoulder to stifle them. "Only in the evenings?" she said against his dressing gown.

Ezra wrapped an arm around her. His blood heated again as scenarios raced through his mind. "Or whenever the mood strikes us."

She raised her head, eyes darkening in the lamplight. "Good."

He didn't know who moved first, only that he was finally kissing her again, his hands on her body that was still half-draped over his. As much as his hands itched to rip away her shift, he kept them on her generous hips, and her heart-shaped arse that he'd been dreaming of grabbing for weeks now. The heat of her skin seared his through the thin material.

Claudia had taken the lead on this. It was important that things moved along at her clip.

He lifted one hand to touch her hair, as soft as he'd imagined it to be. She gave a sigh of pleasure against his lips, and he took the opportunity to kiss a trail down her throat, where her ever-present scent of frankincense lingered. Beneath it was the fragrance of the soap she'd used that morning, and her skin. She gasped again, body gently arching against him. His hips lifted of their own accord in a feeble pantomime of what he really wanted to do to her. With her.

Her hands tugged at his dressing gown again, fussing with the belt loosely tied around his waist. She didn't pull the sides apart all the way, much to his disappointment. He wanted her hands all over him. Instead, she pushed away the fabric from his shoulders as she had done when he first kissed her, sitting up a little to better see him. She traced her fingers over his chest, as if memorizing the lines of his body. Her touch was light, almost innocent, but a shudder still rippled through him.

"Are you all right?" she whispered.

"Of course. Never better." Her hand trailed further down his body, down his chest to his stomach. His lower half was still loosely covered by his robe, but his erection was outlined by the fabric, growing harder with every sweep of her hand over his skin. His blood raced through his veins, so hot he thought he might combust.

And they were still wearing *clothes!*

God only knew how he might explode once he finally saw her breasts or she touched his cock. All of his learned control threatened to leave him where Claudia was concerned. He felt like a young man again, woefully inexperienced and eager to please when it came to her.

Her hand slid under the edge of the dressing gown, grazing over his hip bone. Her warm fingers so close to the part of him that wanted her the most, the knowing half-smile on her lips that he wanted to kiss, her barely covered body so close to his all bordered on torture. As much as it pained him to do so, he reached out to still her hand, grasping it over his clothing.

"Should I not do that?" she asked.

"I very much want you to. But if you do, this will be over before it's begun."

Understanding dawned in her expression, quickly replaced by a smirk. "I don't want the party to end just yet."

An odd sense of relief trickled through Ezra. There had been a small worry at the back of his mind that he would come on too strong, scare her or hurt her in some way. He reached for her, cupping his hand around her cheek, to draw her to him. Their mouths met in a tangle of lips and tongues, breaths mingling. He lowered his hand until his fingers found the strap of her shift and dragged it down her shoulder. She pulled away, dark gaze meeting his as she pushed the rest of her shift, the material bunching around her waist to reveal her full breasts. Ezra's mouth went dry as he took in the sight, better than he imagined. "Wow."

Claudia blushed. "You haven't seen the rest of me yet."

"I'm sure you're stunning." He kissed her again, hand sliding up her body to cup her breast. He kneaded it, tweaking her nipple and drawing a gasp against his lips from her.

She broke the kiss, pressing her forehead against his. Her hand had again found his waist, and slid under his dressing gown.

Making no move to stop her, a groan of pleasure sounded in his throat when her fingers wrapped around his cock. His hips lifted again, thrusting into her hand. Through gritted teeth, he said, "Lie back on the bed with your knees raised."

Her eyes widened, but she obliged, setting her head against the pillows.

Ezra shucked off his robe and tossed it away, not caring where it landed. He shifted, moving down the bed until he was sitting at her knees now pressed together. Her shift had pooled around her waist, hiding what he most wanted to see. It was like a gift he was going to relish unwrapping. He gently urged her knees apart, pressing a kiss to one. He skimmed his hand up her outer thigh, goosebumps raising along her skin under his fingertips. Lowering his head, he kissed her inner thigh, a few inches above her knee, keeping his eyes on her to gauge her reaction.

Claudia's eyes widened slightly, then she gave him the barest of nods.

Ezra grinned. With one hand, he pushed away her shift to reveal her sex, then dipped his head.

Her response was immediate. A small cry escaped her and her thighs tightened a little around his head as his tongue explored her, already wet.

Gripping her hips, he doubled his efforts, her breathy little moans and hands fisting in her hair encouraging him. He found the spot that made her body quiver around him, another harsh, short cry that she quickly muffled by clapping a hand over her mouth. Her body bowed against his face as she came, one of her legs draped over his shoulder and her heel digging into his back. It took every ounce of his self-control not to spend on the bed himself.

When her breath slowed, Ezra kissed her inner thigh, then raised his head. Claudia lay against the pillows, dark hair spread around her, eyes glazed and color high on her cheeks. She had never looked more beautiful or desirable, an erotic artwork come to life. Her gaze met his. "Oh, wow," she murmured. "I didn't know it could be like that."

Pride warred with jealousy over her words. "I try."

"Oh, you did more than that. And it wasn't enough." She pushed her shift down her body, kicking it off the bed so she was fully nude. "Can I be on top?"

The very thought of her riding him ... damn it, he nearly came. "Jesus Christ."

She shrugged. "Not my god."

It should have felt inappropriate to laugh, and yet he could do that with her. "Zeus, then."

She levered herself up on her elbows to shoot him a look. "I'm *Roman*, Ezra."

"Is it bad that I can't remember the Roman equivalents right now?"

"No, I'll forgive you this one." She lifted herself to a sitting position. "You didn't answer my question."

"I thought I did." He cupped her face in his hands and kissed her deeply. Then he took her spot in the middle of the bed.

Claudia grinned, then straddled him, hovering over his body. "There's just one thing," she said.

"I'll give you anything you want," he promised hoarsely.

"Don't get me pregnant."

The statement threw a bit of a damper on his ardor, yet it was a relief to know that one of them could still listen to the voice of reason. It was uncharacteristic of Ezra, who had always been careful and kept a supply of safes in his bedroom at home. "I promise I'll withdraw."

"Thank you."

It was then that she started to lower herself on to his cock, guiding him into her. He gritted his teeth, forcing himself to remain still until he was fully seated inside her. She gave an experimental wiggle of her hips against him that was nearly his undoing, but he held on to his self-control. He let her take the lead, setting a rhythm that he followed.

She rested his hands on his chest for balance.

That was a pleasant weight against him, and he kept his hands on her hips as they moved together. He watched her through heavily lidded eyes, her face a mask of lust, the feel of her body surrounding and covering him better than he could have possibly imagined. He wasn't sure how much time had passed, but Claudia's breathing increased and her rhythm increased, and he knew she was close to another climax. Remembering his promise to her, he concentrated on holding off, waiting and needing for her to finish around him. She did, with a cry muffled by her face being in his neck, her body spasming on his. She leaned against him, completely spent, before he reluctantly nudged her away. "*Claudia.*"

He must have conveyed the urgency in his voice with enough effect, because she rolled off him.

A few seconds later, he spent on the bedspread. For a moment, the only sound in the room was of their breathing, ragged and uneven. When Ezra could move his limbs again, he kicked away the bedspread and pulled the sheet over them. Without a word, she snuggled against him, head against his chest.

CHAPTER 14

Claudia was dimly aware of the brass clock ticking the second away on the other side of the room, perched on the chest of drawers. It was almost in tandem with Ezra's heartbeat thumping under her head, steady and comforting. A reminder that they were very much alive. "Thank you," she said, when she could find her voice.

"I could say the same. I didn't know how much I wanted that with you until it happened." He pressed a kiss to the top of her head and tightened his arms around her. One hand reached out to lazily play with her hair.

"No, I mean thank you for withdrawing. That means a lot to me."

He stilled. "Should I ask? Has that not been respected in the past?"

"It doesn't matter."

He shifted, sitting up a little. Claudia moved to her side to face him, propping herself up on one arm. "Yes, it does," he said firmly. "If this is to continue, you have to understand that I will always listen to you and what you want. Besides that, I don't want children at this stage of my life, either."

"You're very modern in your outlook. I appreciate that. And no, that request wasn't always respected."

"I'm sorry that happened to you." He paused, as if choosing his words carefully. "May I ask you something?"

"Of course. I don't think there are any secrets between us." Did it count as a secret if she simply hadn't brought up particular subjects in the first place?

"Did you have children before?"

"No. I was lucky. I was only betrothed to be married. My parents would have never forgiven me if I became pregnant when I wasn't married."

He was quiet again, and she knew he wanted to ask about Marcus. "You can ask about my betrothed. I'll always answer any questions you have. I trust you." She lightly traced her finger over his chest, drawing a faint shudder of pleasure from him.

"I'm uncertain what I want to know about is appropriate bedroom discussion," he replied.

"What you want to ask about doesn't really have an appropriate time."

His hand squeezed her shoulder. "What happened?"

She sighed, taking some time to collect her thoughts. "There was a fire."

"Oh, Claudia." The anguish in his voice tore at her.

"I was visiting with my betrothed, Marcus. I was friends with his sisters, too." It felt as if she was talking about someone else, reciting her story as if they had been dictated to her. She supposed she *was* a different person now. "Marcus and I had a marriage arranged for us by our parents after my first suitor died. I think both of us were happy to be put together. No." That was wrong. "I don't know if we were *happy*, exactly, but we weren't put out by the arrangement. It wasn't a love match, but I liked him well enough and I thought he liked me, too." She couldn't even remember what he looked like, just that he'd had dark hair. She wouldn't be able to describe anything else about him. "Marcus's sisters went out to the market, or visit a friend. I don't remember, exactly. The point is that they were out of the house and we were alone, and … well."

"You got up to what young people do when they're alone," Ezra translated.

It was awkward to admit, but true. "Yes." She felt a blush creep up her neck admitting that, but she thought Ezra wouldn't mind. "Night fell and his sisters didn't return, which wasn't unusual. They had other friends they liked to visit. His parents weren't home, either. It got dark, and Marcus lit a candle." She had to backtrack, explain Marcus's family home. "The house only had a couple of rooms. It was very small, very little privacy, not like the houses of today."

"The candle," Ezra said, voice tinged with sadness.

"It was only a stub and it caught fire on the table it was resting on. Wood, of course. The rest of the house went up in flames almost immediately. It had been a hot and dry summer, hardly any rain …" To her surprise, angry tears clogged her throat. She hadn't cried over her own death in centuries. It took her a moment to speak again. "Marcus had left the house to get water from the well outside before his parents returned. I was at the back of the corner of the room. I think I'd been napping on his sleeping pallet. I didn't wake up before the house was on fire and I couldn't leave. I opened the window—I suppose you would call it a shutter—and he saw me trying to get out, but it was too small and too high up for me to fit through. He saw me struggling. He didn't try to save me." Her voice broke, and a few tears slid down her cheeks as her centuries-old rage returned. "Marcus saw me try to get out. He looked me in the eye and did nothing. He yelled for help, then turned around and ran away. He was supposed to love me, and he left me to die."

"Claudia," said Ezra.

She soldiered on. "I don't want to talk about the act of dying. I don't think I ever will. I remember walking around the ruins of the house after the fire was extinguished knowing I hadn't survived the fire. I knew I was a ghost." She'd hated using that word to describe herself before she was resurrected, preferring to call herself a spirit. It sounded so much less sinister. "Everyone was angry with Marcus because he left me in the house and didn't try to put out the fire. My family was devastated. I couldn't stay in Londinium but couldn't figure out how to leave this plane. So, when he was driven out by guilt and shame, I followed him. We ended up in what's now Liverpool. He built a small house of his own there. I stayed with him until he became convinced that he was being haunted by me and left it."

"You *were* haunting him," Ezra pointed out gently.

"I think haunting implies I meant to scare him, and I didn't. I just didn't know where else to go. I didn't want to follow him again, so I stayed where I was."

"Is that Merritt's former flat?"

"A lot of things were built on the site over the years, but yes. Technically, the one across the corridor from his."

"And here I am, dragging you across London while a fire-breathing demon stomps across the city. My God, Julian's house was on fire!" Ezra clutched her to him, almost too tightly.

She appreciated his concern, but peeled herself away just enough to breathe more comfortably. "If I was terrified of fire, I would have returned to Liverpool by now. Or checked into a hotel."

"How would you know about renting a room at a hotel?"

"How difficult could it be? Doesn't one walk into a hotel and ask for a room?"

"Yes, but there's the matter of money. You've forgotten about that a few times."

An odd sense of relief trickled through Claudia at the change in subject, even though she knew Ezra was playing along in an attempt to make her feel better. "Not lately. I haven't wandered off after helping myself to an apple at the market in months." Ezra had been mortified, in a hilarious sort of way, when that happened. She smiled at the memory. Just as quickly, her mirth was gone. "Thank you for listening to me."

"You don't ever have to thank me for that."

"I've never told anyone before."

"Not Merritt?"

"Merritt is too polite to ask those sorts of questions to random spirits. He's always respected them for their reasons for staying on this plane and doesn't pry."

Ezra was quiet, probably mulling over the politest way to ask his next question. "And you don't know why you stayed here?"

"Perhaps I missed the window of opportunity to cross over, or I didn't know what it looked like." She snuggled against him. "Now, I like to think I stayed because I was waiting for you."

She hadn't meant to say that, although now that she had, she didn't regret it. Ezra didn't reply, only tucked the linen sheet a little tighter around them.

Sunlight filtered through a small gap in the drapes, landing squarely across Ezra's eyes. He blinked, then glanced at the brass clock ticking away on the opposite side of the room. It looked to be nearing nine o'clock, unusually late for him to sleep in. He glanced at the woman curled up beside him, still blissfully asleep. Warmth and affection surged inside him at the sight, a reassurance that the night before hadn't been an incredible dream. The memories were enough to arouse him all over again, but he tamped down the urges. He kissed her cheek, which earned him a sleepy, unintelligible murmur before she shifted her head on the pillow.

He crept out of bed, taking care not to disturb her. His dressing gown was on the floor, which he picked up and slipped on. When he let himself out of the room, he saw the door to Julian's was open. From downstairs, he could hear the clatter of a coffee cup being placed on a saucer, and guessed Julian had already served himself breakfast. He had probably helped himself to Ezra's old art supplies, too.

Ezra washed and dressed before descending the stairs. He found Julian at the kitchen table, also dressed, another oddity.

"Good morning," Julian said, sounding more cheerful than he had in days. "I've already been out. Our demon friend made the front pages of the *Times* and the *London Owl*." He held up copies of the newspapers.

That bit of information put a damper on Ezra's mood but didn't destroy it. "Should I expect a barrage of reporters at my door today?"

"It's possible. If they do appear, I'll speak to them." Julian tilted his chair back and took a long, languorous sip of coffee. "We've got it all worked out how we'll deal with this thing. It should be fine."

More of Ezra's good mood evaporated at the casual way Julian handled this. "A demon stomped through my garden last night and scared the shit out of the neighborhood, bastions of reporters may well show up on my doorstep any second, and you're wrecking my mother's kitchen chairs while you smirk at me over this?"

Julian stopped tilting his chair, returning all four legs to the tiled floor with a thump. "We've established that the demon will listen to me. We should have tried ordering it back to hell or wherever it came from at the Thames," Julian explained. "My artwork hasn't been moved yet and is still aboard the floating gallery. I'm going to host a performance art piece tonight, the likes of which the London art world has never seen, order Spring-Heeled Jack back to whence he came, and then I get to be revered as a true artist while London is rid of the demon. How is this not a brilliant idea?"

"I don't remember you ever being this organized after a night of drinking," Ezra said suspiciously.

"I had a single bottle of red wine on an empty stomach, which is hardly anything to my constitution. I had a good sleep last night, too. Did you? Your bedroom door was open and you were nowhere to be found this morning." Julian smirked at him over the rim of his cup.

Ezra didn't rise to the bait. "I slept better than I have in months, thank you. Is there any coffee left?"

Julian gestured to the tall silver pot on the table in front of him. "It's two-thirds full. Help yourself."

"It's my fucking coffee anyway," he grumbled before fixing himself a cup and taking a seat opposite Julian.

"So, you spent the night with Claudia," said Julian, getting straight to the point.

"I did. And it's not a subject that's up for discussion."

"Understood. I'm just glad to see that you're finally

following your instincts. She's a sweet girl. God knows why she's enamored with you."

"What the hell is that supposed to mean?"

"I mean, you do everything you can to keep everyone at arm's length, including me, so imagine how surprised I was when you show up at a London railway with this odd girl you can't keep your eyes off of and can't stop touching, yet you wouldn't follow an instinct that a blind bat could sense you have. It's nice to see you happy, is all. You deserve some happiness."

Ezra wasn't sure what he'd been expecting to hear. It hadn't been that. Come to think of it, he'd always taken every opportunity he could to be close to Claudia, even before he'd figured out that he was falling in love with her. "Thank you, I suppose." *Huh. I've never been in love before. So this is what it feels like?*

Julian shrugged. "You're welcome." He poured another cup of coffee. "Look, I do apologize for this mess we're in. I appreciate you and Claudia helping me. Claudia—God damn, I get why you adore her. She's incredibly smart. You don't find Latin-speaking experts in demonology in polite society that often, do you?"

"I — no, you don't."

"You two could've fucked off back to Liverpool and let me deal with this thing on my own, but you didn't. You've been better friends to me than I have to you."

"Does this mean the great Julian Smythe is having a change of heart about himself? Does this mean you'll take off all those brass and copper tiles from your house? They're hideous, if you must know."

Affronted, Julian replied, "They make my house look like a cog, which is the point. I'm trying to convey that we're all cogs in a pointless machine."

"Are we, though? We were both born into the kind of wealth that means neither of us has to work."

"Ah ha!" Julian looked at him in triumph. "My artwork counts as work. I'm actually creating something, even you consider much of it is silly. You should expand your tastes. The most recent work in your studio is dated five years ago. Has it really been five years since you stopped making art?"

Ezra hated that Julian had a point. "I occasionally invest in art shows in Liverpool, so I'm still involved. There's more recent work at my home, but nothing meant to be viewed by the public."

Slightly mollified, Julian leaned back in his seat. "I'll accept that. I didn't know there was much of an art community in Liverpool."

"I helped sponsor a couple of exhibits at the Walker Gallery recently, so yes, there is. There are huge collectives across England, not just in London. You might enjoy seeking them out sometime."

Any rejoinder Julian might have offered was interrupted by a knock at the front door.

Ezra sighed, knowing who was probably on the other side of it. "I hope that's a reporter from a respectable publication," he grumbled.

The man waiting on the other side of the door looked respectable enough, at least. His short-clipped hair was silver under the brim of his hat, a sharp contrast to his youthful face, which looked to be only a few years older than Ezra. The cut of his charcoal coat indicated it was bespoke, as did his trousers. Behind him, a small ornithopter was parked in the front garden pathway. Ezra appreciated that he'd had the consideration not to leave it on the grass. "May I help you?" he asked.

"Good morning. I'm looking for Ezra Thaddeus or

Julian Smythe. Are you one of them?" the visitor asked brightly.

"The former. Who are you?"

"Oliver Milton, from the *London Owl.*"

Ezra inwardly groaned. Trust a tabloid to show up first thing in the morning on his doorstep. He had a feeling a *Times* reporter might be a little more considerate of the time. "What can I help you with, Mr. Milton?"

The reporter flashed him a brilliant smile. "Have you seen the front pages of the papers this morning?"

Ezra pinched the bridge of his nose between two fingers. "Yes. You may as well come in." He held open the door for him.

Mr. Milton stepped inside and removed his hat. "Is there somewhere we could talk?"

"The kitchen. Julian's already made a pot of coffee. Julian!" Ezra called. "We have company."

Julian stuck his head out the kitchen doorway, looking far too delighted for someone who had unleashed a demon across the city. "Good morning. Who shall I say is calling?" he asked, excitement in his voice.

"Oliver Milton, from the *Owl,*" Ezra replied.

"I see the *Owl* has taken an interest in art. Great news to hear! Julian Smythe." He ducked back into the kitchen. "Coffee?"

"I'd love some, thank you." The reporter followed Ezra into the kitchen and took off his coat, draping it over the back of a chair. His waistcoat matched his trousers, covering a pressed white linen shirt stained with black ink on the cuffs. Definitely a writer. "So, Mr. Smythe, I did write about a creature seen fleeing your neighborhood a couple of nights ago, shortly after your art gallery opening experienced a small fire. Did you see that?"

"I don't usually read the *Owl,* but I did see a headline

to that effect, at least about a creature allegedly stomping his way through my house," Julian replied smoothly. "It was greatly exaggerated, even for a paper of the *Owl's* reputation."

If Milton was insulted by the slight, he didn't let on. "I didn't write that piece, but I am following up on it. The creature was spotted here again last night. What is it, exactly?"

"An illusion I'm working on for an impromptu exhibit."

Oh, God. Ezra fought the urge to scrub his hands over his face in frustration. He and Julian should have spent more time discussing what to say to reporters instead of bantering about Claudia and why he was letting his artistic skills atrophy. "Julian," he muttered, hoping he put enough warning into his voice.

Julian ignored him. "We've had a few false starts with the illusion, but I'm confident that we can successfully pull off this exhibit."

Milton regarded him thoughtfully under a sweep of light-colored lashes. "Interesting. A number of witnesses in your neighborhood and this one have claimed that they saw a demon of some kind, breathing fire and vapor. One of my colleagues has called it the return of Spring-Heeled Jack. Are you familiar with the legend?"

"Both of us are. Utter rubbish," Julian announced. "It's the mark of a good artist when the witnesses question what they've seen."

"Are you an artist or an illusionist?" Milton asked. He removed a stub of a pencil and small notebook from his trouser pocket, not unlike the one Merritt Sloan always had on his person.

"They're the same thing with different mediums. I prefer to call myself an artist. It's more encompassing."

"Aside from the damage to Julian's house, which is

being repaired, this illusion hasn't been a nuisance or dangerous," Ezra lied.

"I'd argue fire is always dangerous." Milton swiftly replied. To Julian, he asked, "When do you plan on pulling off this illusion or performance art, whatever you want to call it? I'd love to see it."

"Tonight, on the deck of the same ship housing my recent art opening," Julian announced.

Oh, God.

Milton perked up. "Truly?"

"Truly?" echoed Ezra.

Julian ignored Ezra. "Yes. It will be on the upper deck of the ship, although I fear I won't be able to offer the same refreshments as I did at the opening. It's strictly for observation and a chance to say one was present at the time."

The creaking of floorboards above them told Ezra that Claudia was awake. "Excuse me, I have to see to my wife," he said, standing. Julian raised an eyebrow but didn't comment on Ezra's choice of words. Despite the gravity of their situation, Ezra couldn't help but notice how he liked referring to Claudia as his wife.

"Do you think your wife would be willing to speak to me?" Milton asked.

"Doubtful, but I'll send her your regards." Should Ezra bring some breakfast to Claudia? He thought it might be polite. He quickly poured the remains of the coffee pot into a cup, noting it was the last clean one in the cupboard. He met Claudia at the top of the stairs, coming out of the bathroom. She wore an old dressing gown she must have pulled from the wardrobe, the garment swallowing her. Taking care not to spill the coffee, Ezra kissed her by way of greeting. To his relief, she kissed him back, melting into him. At least she didn't seem to regret their night together.

"Do we have company?" she whispered.

"A reporter from the *London Owl*, coming to follow up on reports of a demon in my garden last night. It's on the front page of the morning papers, and will no doubt be on the front pages of the evening papers, too."

"Do you think the *Owl* ever writes about animals? I'd read a newspaper that published stories about them."

"I'm certain they've published a few lurid pieces of about brutal animal attacks. Probably not about cat fanciers' shows."

She stared at him, agog, then took the coffee cup from his hand. "There are cat fancier shows and you didn't tell me about them? As in, people show off their cats?"

"Yes, but that's not my point."

"And anyone can attend these shows? Can you pet the cats?"

"Yes. Claudia, I'm trying to explain to you that Julian is setting up a viewing for the public, on the Thames, where is going to send that demon back to the underworld tonight."

She wasn't disturbed by this information. "Well, of course he is. We discussed doing that last night. We probably should have tried that in the first place. Not the part about doing it for an audience, though, although that sort of makes sense since he was summoned with one."

"And what if it doesn't work?"

"We know it will listen to Julian. We also know that the best way to return it to the underworld is to recreate the circumstances it was summoned in the first place. I'm fairly certain tonight's attempt will be successful." A furrow appeared between her brows. "I have to believe that. That poor thing is probably confused and scared."

"You're calling a demon on the loose a 'poor thing'?"

Her reply was indignant. "Yes. He's confused, he's sort

of stupid, he just wants to go home. He hasn't hurt anyone and he's had plenty of opportunities to do so. I know what it feels like to be trapped on a plane without a way to leave."

Guilt twanged through Ezra. She was right. He remembered her sleepy words the night before, that she thought she might have been left on the earth to wait for him. If she hadn't, he still was grateful she was here. "That's a good point and aside from the ballroom fire, he hasn't harmed anyone."

"Children of mischievous gods rarely do."

"You've met a lot of the offspring of deities?"

She shrugged. "It's possible."

"Do you think your Roman religion might be the true one? What if everyone else is merely wasting their time worshipping the wrong gods?" That notion had crossed his mind a couple of times since meeting her. The matter of their unexpected guest had fallen by the wayside, even though it had to be one of the worst possible times to start seriously pondering what happened after death.

She looked thoughtful, taking a few seconds to compose her answer. She took a deep swallow of coffee. "I don't know. Perhaps there are many versions of the after-life, and you go to the one you're drawn to. I wouldn't know for sure and it could just be a matter of groups having different names for the same gods. I don't believe my people and the ancient Greeks were the only ones to do that."

Ezra recalled his quip the night before. "Like Zeus."

She rolled her eyes. "Like Jupiter."

The discussion of the afterlife also reminded him of their conversation after they'd made love. "Thank you for telling me everything last night," he said quietly. He wrapped her free hand in his. "I know it must have taken a lot to talk about after so long."

"Thank you for not being weird about it. It felt good to tell someone."

Laughter downstairs reminded him that they still had a visitor, albeit one Ezra wanted to get out of his house and that visitor had been told a lie that Claudia should know about. "Before I forget, I told the reporter that you're my wife. If the subject comes up tonight— and I fully expect him to appear at the ship tonight— please, just go along with it."

"That won't be a hardship." She kissed him, a tease that brought a groan to his throat. He wished he could kick out Julian and Milton so they could have some privacy. "I'm going to take a bath."

"I wish I could join you."

"We'll have to try that out when we get home." She drained the last of her coffee, and Ezra took her cup. "I'd like to say I won't be long in the water, but that would be a lie."

CHAPTER 15

THE EVENING NEWSPAPERS were displayed in what seemed like every other storefront, or perhaps Claudia was more attuned to them. Almost every front page had something printed about the demon, whether it was announcing the return of Spring-Heeled Jack or deriding people for becoming hysterical over nothing. The *London Owl* had a profile on Julian, which irritated him after he saw it. "Damn it, why couldn't I have spoken to a reporter from the *Times* or *Manchester Guardian* first?" he groused in front of a news kiosk. It was a short tower with a pointed red top about Claudia's height. The machine slowly spun around, showing off the newspapers held in place with heavy brass rods. A bored-looking attendant stood nearby, smoking a pipe.

"Probably because those newspapers employ reporters who research their work first," Ezra replied. He deposited a coin in a slot on one of the racks, then lifted a rod and removed a copy of the *Owl*. He held it out to Julian. "Don't tell me you're going to pass by a paper that has an article about you on the front page."

"Of course, I'm not. My mother will want to read it, even if it's a rubbish paper."

"Well, you've made the front page of the *Evening Herald*, too."

That perked up Julian a little. "I did?"

Oliver Milton had apparently been intrigued by Julian's lies that morning and offered to bring an audience to the floating gallery on the Thames, preceded by supper at a restaurant, something Claudia was looking forward to despite the dangers that lay ahead of them that night. After Milton had finally left the house, she, Ezra, and Julian spent the rest of the afternoon poring over the notes from Matilda, running over every scenario where something could go wrong.

Ezra's lips were thinned as he watched Julian shove newspapers into his battered leather satchel.

Julian had gone out of his way to look the part of a stereotypical artist. While his clothes were obviously well-made, they were damaged with ink and paint, cuffs frayed. His leather boots were the sort a coal miner might wear, out of place in an art gallery. His hat was set at an angle, a huge, jaunty red-dyed feather sticking out of it that warred with the pink ones on Claudia's own hat for ostentatiousness.

At least she was wearing a skirt. She would fit in with the restaurant's patrons.

They hailed a steam cab to take them to the restaurant, the place a short walk from the Thames' floating gallery. Oliver Milton waited for them, six or seven well-dressed people seated with him at a large table in the back of the restaurant. His silvery-gray hair shone in the electric lamplight, belying the rest of him, which couldn't be older than his mid-thirties. A small, leather-bound notebook rested on the table in front of him next to a glass of red wine. He heartily clapped Julian on the back. "This is Julian Smythe, the man of art and illusions himself, ready to show London what it takes to lure Spring-Heeled Jack back to the depth of hell," he announced.

Preening under the attention, Julian greeted everyone.

"Let me introduce you to Mr. and Mrs. Thaddeus, friends of Julian's," Milton said, although few people paid attention to Ezra and Claudia.

With a start, she remembered that Ezra told Milton she was his wife. She felt a blush creep up her cheeks, and a smile spread across her face. She wouldn't mind being Mrs. Claudia Drusilla Lucius Thaddeus. When she glanced at Ezra, he had a thoughtful look on his face, like he was imagining it, too. He squeezed her hand. Claudia promptly forgot the names of everyone around the table, mostly reporters from the *Owl* and other newspapers. She took a seat at the end next to Ezra, who made a fuss of helping her with her coat and hat. A couple of waiters appeared after everyone was seated, a large cart between them loaded down with plates of the first course.

"Prawn soup," whispered Ezra in her ear.

She perked up. She'd recently discovered that she loved prawns. Throughout the meal, she discovered that she also loved blanched green vegetables in a spicy sauce whose flavors she couldn't pick out, and mutton carved into star shapes and drenched in gravy. She and Ezra were given a small dish of olives to share. She was content to eat while everyone else peppered Julian with questions about his art, occasionally asking Ezra questions when they remembered his presence. Claudia was largely ignored, which she preferred. She wouldn't be able to hold a conversation with any of these people.

It wasn't until the dessert dishes were cleared away and everyone gathered drained the last of their wine that

Milton stood up. "I've already settled our account." A few half-hearted protests from his friends followed, but he waved them away. "It's half-eight and nearly full dark. I think it's time to see Julian pull off this piece of performance art, isn't it?"

Julian, at the opposite end of the table next to Milton, looked stricken for half a second before his face split in a grin. "I can hardly wait to demonstrate it to you."

"Will there be an opportunity to see the rest of your works? I understand they're still aboard the ship," one of Milton's friends asked. His voice was deep and loose.

Claudia had spotted him refilling his glass more than anyone else. For a few seconds, she wished she could tell everyone present what they faced tonight and recommend they be sober.

"I don't see why not," Julian replied.

"I've heard a great deal of your work. Daring, they're calling it, but I'd like to see that for myself."

"And you shall have that chance," Milton promised. He gave a knowing look to Julian. "Let's go."

CLAUDIA AND EZRA tagged behind the crowd as they strolled through the streets to the art gallery's dock. It was the first time they'd had a chance to see London without a demon at their heels, and Claudia was a little sad their visit was so rushed. She had been looking forward to seeing how Londinium changed. Perhaps they could do that on another visit. She glanced at Ezra, whose vision was trained on the group a few paces ahead of him. Tight-lipped, obviously nervous about what lay ahead, he looked back at her, expression softening.

"This has to work," he whispered in her hair.

"I hope so."

One of Milton's friends, the drunk one, turned around at the sound of her voice and gave her a leer.

"Supper was good," she said.

"I'm surprised you ate that much," Ezra replied, shooting the man daggers. He quickly turned around and picked up his pace to match that of his friends.

"I'm fond of good food. You should know that sex gives me an appetite."

Ezra gave a strange cough that sounded almost choked. When he recovered, he said, "I do admire your propensity to be blunt. I appreciate both of those things, too. With you," he quickly added.

"You, as well." Hopefully, when this was all over tonight, they could take their time and get to know each other's bodies more. She wondered how she would tell Merritt about this change in their relationship. She couldn't be certain he would take the news that well. He viewed her almost as a little sister who needed to be protected.

She could smell the Thames before she saw it, brackish and foul. If the others noticed, they didn't let on. Perhaps they were used to living with the stink. Her good mood evaporated when the floating hulk of a gallery came into view, stomach twisting on itself when she saw the people gathered, their voices excited murmurs. By Claudia's rough estimation, there had to be at least fifty or sixty people in attendance.

At the sight of Milton's entourage, a few pointed them out.

Oh, gods above and below. They were here for a show. How the hell did they find out about it? Had it been printed in all of the papers? As they threaded their way through the crowd, a few people called out greetings to Milton, or one of his associates, occasionally Julian himself. Claudia recognized a few people from Julian's gallery opening. She wished she knew a little more about Oliver Milton to understand why he warranted such attention. Were reporters that famous, or had the story of the demon spread that quickly in so little time? She had never thought about how fast news could spread in the modern age.

Ezra squeezed her hand, gave her a reassuring smile as they boarded the ship's gangplank.

It was empty save for their group, and dark, with only a few lamps turned to low that cast shadows over the remaining artwork. A few pieces were missing, probably sold given that Julian didn't seem concerned about their absence.

"Will there be an opportunity to view the gallery after the performance?" one of the men asked.

Julian shrugged. "I don't see why not."

His words were flip, surer than Claudia knew him to be. There was a faint tremble to his voice, lines bracketing his eyes and mouth that hadn't been there before. They walked through the gallery rooms, and up two flights of stairs to the upper deck. Claudia's stomach roiled, and she thought she might be in danger of losing her supper on the floor. What a shame to waste such a lovely meal.

The crowd on the shore broke into applause and cheers when they reached the upper deck. Julian looked a little panicked at the sound, then pasted a smile on his face. "I don't think I can do this," he said through gritted teeth to her and Ezra.

"You can and you will," Ezra snapped. "This can't go on."

On the shore, a woman stood under a glowing street

lamp, yellow light bathing her cloud of dark hair, noticeable by her lack of hat. She looked familiar. Claudia squinted at her; was that … Matilda? Had the witch—or daughter of a god, whoever she claimed to be—attended? As if she sensed Claudia's scrutiny, Matilda waved an ungloved hand in her direction. Claudia waved back. The sight of the witch put her at ease, oddly enough. Matilda had claimed not to be an effective seer, but perhaps she was here if she knew everyone was going to come out of this in one piece, with Spring-Heeled Jack safely tucked back in the underworld. She started to whisper in Ezra's ear that Matilda was here, but Julian interrupted her.

"I shall require everyone but my trusted associates to stand at the back of the ship," he commanded.

"Aft," Milton corrected him.

"I beg your pardon?"

"The back of a ship is called 'aft.'"

"I'm an artist, not a sailor," Julian replied. "Everyone, to the aft of the ship." Milton remained rooted in place. "You, too, Oliver."

Milton looked surprised at the order, but obeyed.

Julian glanced at Ezra and Claudia. He had a beseeching look in his eyes, plain even in the darkness. "Come with me."

Steeling herself, Claudia and Ezra walked alongside Julian until they reached the front of the ship. The bow, she recalled. A former sailor had once taken up residence in the flat she'd haunted, albeit briefly. Come to think of it, she couldn't remember which side of a boat was portside or starboard.

"This better work," Ezra muttered.

"Oh, God, I hope so. I suppose it's too much to hope for that thing to go back to hell on its own," said Julian. He pulled out the sheet of foolscap from Matilda's shop, now well-creased from near-constant handling. He took a deep breath. "Before I start, I should tell you that I'm very sorry for all of this. I didn't intend for it to happen."

"No one expects to summon a demon when you're simply trying to sell statues of nude horses," Ezra replied.

"Aren't horses usually nude, anyway?" Claudia asked.

"Ezra's having a go at me, and I deserve some of it. At least I'm still trying with my art. The next time I see you, I expect to see at least one completed masterpiece in your possession. You have a lot of talent. I hope you don't squander it."

Ezra's eyes widened at the compliment. It took a few seconds for him to find his voice. "Thank you."

"I mean it. You can go ahead and poke fun at my house and its tilework all you want, but I'd rather be a pretentious try-hard than a layabout living off an inheritance."

Ezra opened his mouth to argue, but Julian held up his hand.

"I have a trust, too, yes. No need to point it out. If you are going to take any advice from me, it should be to explore your talents and push them to the limits. Even if you end up summoning a demon."

"Understood. Thank you for the life advice," Ezra replied.

"Come here." Julian shoved the paper in his pocket and held out his arms. "Just in case I fuck this up and the ship tips over, I'd like us to go out on good terms."

"God damn it, I forgot to ask about life vests," Ezra grumbled.

Claudia couldn't help but feel a little intrigued at the notion, and nearly blurted out "What's a life vest?" but halted herself in time. Instead, she let Julian hug her, and a second later, Ezra joined in.

"I love you two," said Julian. "You don't have to say anything in response. Just know that you've been great friends to me throughout this, when you could've bolted back to Liverpool and resumed your lives." He let them go and took a couple of steps away from them, as if the short distance would keep them safe while he recited his spell. Taking a deep breath, he launched into it, the Latin words flowing off his tongue with far better fluency than only a couple of days ago.

Ezra lifted Claudia's chin with his finger, gaze meeting hers. His voice was quiet, serious. "In case we don't get through this, know that I love you."

Claudia hadn't been expecting that. Her heart skipped a couple of beats and her knees went weak. She had to hold on to Ezra to keep from sliding to the deck in a heap. She had never expected to hear those words, never thought she would ever fall in love herself ... She blinked in surprise. "I love you, too." She did. She loved how he'd taught her how to live in the nineteenth century, how he enjoyed talking with her like she was his equal, how he offered comfort whenever she needed it. How she first came to depend on his touch when she was learning how to walk and speak again, and then later craved it. How their friendship naturally evolved into what it was now, how right that had felt.

"You do?" Ezra said in surprise.

"Why wouldn't I?"

Julian's voice, rising in volume as he recited the spell, was nearly a shout. "*Praecipio tibi ut compareas coram domino tuo, ostende te et revertere unde venisti!*" An order for the demon to appear before its master and return to the underworld, spoken with a confidence that Claudia never would have expected to hear from an English-speaking artist.

Screams sounded from the shore. Everyone aboard the ship turned to look at the crowded docks, at the giant cloven-hoofed beast that had appeared under a street lamp. Confusion crossed its face, and it opened its mouth to let out a fiery screech. Even from their perch on the upper deck, the scent of sulfur was overwhelming.

The beast locked eyes with Julian. With a swift, horrifying leap that defied logic and gravity, it jumped to the ship, climbing up its railings and posts until it crawled to the upper deck. "Fuck," muttered Julian, unable to tear his eyes off the demon.

"Spectacular!" crowed one of the men at the aft. A light smattering of applause filled the air from the dock. If Claudia didn't know the true origin of the creature, she would have been impressed, too.

"*Ad inferos quo tu pertinent* ," said Julian, pointing at the bow's railing. Back to the underworld where you belong.

"*Aqua*," prompted Claudia. "Through the water. Tell him."

"*Aqua*," repeated Julian, still pointing. The demon looked at it, reluctance on his face. "Claudia, how do I say, 'go home'?"

Before Claudia could translate the phrase, the demon gave a final bellow, smoke and flames issuing from its nostrils into the night sky. Bouncing away, it leapt off the front of the ship, exploding in a ball of white light not unlike the one in which it had arrived. Claudia, Ezra, and Julian rushed to the railing and leaned over. The light hovered over the water, the scents of fire and brimstone nearly unbearable. Her stomach heaved and she was again in danger of being sick. Then it fell into the river with a hearty splash.

Claudia stared at the spot where it dove in, hardly daring to believe her eyes. "Gods above and below," she murmured in wonder.

"I think you did it, Julian," said Ezra.

Julian didn't speak. He didn't tear his eyes off the dark water, as if was worried the creature would return. Finally, he straightened and loosened his grip on the railing. Turning around to face Milton and his friends at the other end of the ship, he held up his hands in triumph. He pasted a smile on his face that would have looked genuine to anyone who didn't know him as well as Claudia and Ezra. "What did you think?" he shouted.

Cheers erupted from the men, then the dock. Milton and his friends returned to the bow to congratulate him on a well-done performance and ask how he did it. Julian shrugged and looked away at the water. "Obviously, I can't tell you how I pulled it off. That was real fire, and my illusion has already caused property damage. I couldn't possibly influence someone less experienced into trying such a thing," Julian announced. He glanced at Claudia and Ezra before turning back to the crowd. "Of course, if anyone is interested in looking at my less-fiery work, I have some pieces still displayed below deck. The gallery curator has been generous to permit an impromptu exhibit this evening, if you'll follow me. You'll have to forgive the lighting this time. I didn't have a chance to set it to my preferences." He led the group to the nearest set of stairs. To Ezra and Claudia, he asked, "Are you coming or headed back to the house?"

They exchanged a glance. Ezra had shadows under his eyes and Claudia knew she had to have them, too. "We'll go home," she said.

Ezra nodded in approval.

"All right, go be boring then. I can't promise I'll return tonight, though."

"Do what you need to do, Julian," Ezra replied breezily. Taking Claudia's arm, he led her down the stairs, behind the throng of Julian's adoring fans or sycophants. She wasn't sure which.

The smell of sulfur had nearly dissipated when they reached the dock, replaced with the ever-present malodorous fragrance of the Thames. A few people pushed past them to see Julian's exhibit, but one familiar dark-haired woman stood under a street lamp as she did while the demon was summoned. Her eyes met Claudia's, and she smiled. "Matilda," she said in greeting.

The witch walked away from her spot, the breeze picking up a few strands of her unbound hair. "It's a pleasure to see you again."

"Did you know Julian was going to ..." Claudia composed herself before she could say 'summon the demon.' "Put on a performance this evening?"

"It was mentioned in most of the evening papers."

"I mean, did you *know*?" Claudia pressed.

"I had a notion your friend would be successful, but I wanted to be certain. I also wanted to be present to see Spring-Heeled Jack in the flesh, so to speak. Even if he wasn't really Spring-Heeled Jack. I've so rarely had the opportunity to see stupid, lower-level demons in my lifetime."

"What about smart demons?" Ezra asked.

The question reminded Claudia of her manners. "Ezra, this is Matilda. She owns the bookshop we talked about. Matilda, this is ..."

"I know who he is and who he is to you."

"Of course." Matilda had claimed to be a poor seer, but Claudia doubted that one needed to have any kind of preternatural ability to see how she and Ezra felt about one another. *He loves me!* she thought excitedly. Just as she loved him.

"There's no chance of anything else escaping tonight, is there?" Ezra asked. He regarded Matilda thoughtfully, undoubtedly remembering that Claudia told him she was an immortal creature from her own time.

"I don't think so," Matilda replied. She bowed her head a little. "To answer your question, I have not seen a smart demon in my lifetime, nor is there an opportunity for anything else of the sort to make its way to this plane. Now, I have to take my leave, if you'll excuse me. It was nice to meet you, Mr. Thaddeus, and good to see you again, Claudia."

Claudia and Ezra said their goodbyes, and the witch sauntered away without so much as a look over her shoulder.

"She's from Roman London," Ezra said, more to himself.

"Yes."

He ticked items off his fingers. "So, now I can say I've met a necromancer, two witches, and a demon."

"And a vampire."

"I haven't met the vampire yet. Merritt hasn't introduced us."

"And me," Claudia added.

His expression softened. "And you. I meant it aboard the ship. I love you and I will for the rest of my life."

Claudia's heart thundered against her ribs at his confession. "I love you, too. I think I have since you helped me walk across your parlor for the first time."

He laced his fingers through hers as if he was afraid she might blow away in the breeze. "I've never been in love before. You'll have to show me what to do."

"Gods above, neither have I. We'll have to figure it out together."

Heedless of any audience nearby, Ezra kissed her, something Claudia would never tire of. He wrapped an arm around her, and they walked away from the river.

EPILOGUE

THREE MONTHS later

The stone drive that led to Ivy and Merritt's house was lined with flowers in full bloom. Ezra knew there would be more behind the house. His late father, Edwin, had prized his gardens, and Ivy had maintained them since his death. The house looked inviting, too. It was lived in and loved, now that Merritt had taken up residence in it since he married Ivy, instead of cold and forbidding as it did after Edwin died. It hadn't taken them long to resettle when they returned from their extended honeymoon across Europe.

Nervousness bloomed in Ezra's stomach at the thought of seeing Merritt. He and Claudia had alluded to their new relationship through letters, uncertain how to divulge it without too many details or invoking Merritt's ire. The necromancer saw Claudia as someone to protect, and he'd seen Ezra at his conniving worst. Ezra had no idea how Merritt would handle seeing him and Claudia as a couple. An *engaged* couple, he thought wryly. Claudia had said an enthusiastic yes to his asking her to marry him a few days

"

prior. He hoped it would be a pleasant surprise for Merritt and Ivy. Most of all, he hoped he wasn't about to be beaten into a bloody pulp after Merritt laid eyes on him for the first time in months and found out what had happened in his absence. The door opened before Ezra could raise its heavy iron and brass knocker.

Ivy stood before them in the foyer, brilliantly attired in a pink and yellow dress. A pink rose was fixed in her dark hair, artfully arranged on top of her head. Her face split into a smile when she saw them. "Thank you for visiting," she said, throwing her arms around him in a hug. "It's been an age!" She let him go to hug Claudia. "You look well."

"Thank you. So do you."

Ezra and Claudia stepped inside the foyer. Claudia unpinned her sunhat. "How were your travels?" he asked.

"Wonderful, and we will certainly visit Spain again. Merritt!" Ivy called. "They're here!"

Ezra tensed.

Claudia shot him a quick smile, taking his hand and following Ivy through the house.

Merritt waited for them in the parlor. He was deeply tanned, a testament to a good holiday. He looked at Claudia and Ezra, hands still clasped together, before he finally spoke. "So, this has happened."

"Merritt," began Ivy.

Ezra interrupted her. "I adore her."

Merritt nodded. "I see."

"Are you going to stand in our way?"

Merritt looked affronted at the question. "Of course not. You're both adults. I can't say I'm thrilled with the speed of this development, but I know Claudia better than most people. I believe her letters and her words when she says she's happy with you. The only other person I can say

I know better than her is Ivy, who has assured me you're a good man."

Ezra held his breath. "So, you're not going to kill me."

"It would be the height of hypocrisy for me to do so, considering I proposed to Ivy before she was out of mourning."

Something in him unknotted and relaxed. It was important to him and Claudia to have Merritt's blessing. "Thank you."

"For what? Not killing you? I'm already pestered enough by ghosts without adding another in the mix." Despite the morbid subject, Merritt smiled.

"You wouldn't, anyway," Claudia piped up.

"No. I want both of you to be happy, and if being together makes you happy, well, I'll support it," said Merritt. To Ezra, he asked, "I hope you'll do the right thing by her."

Ezra felt a smile spread across his face. "I already asked her. She said yes." He didn't think the giddiness of hearing her say that would ever wear off.

"That's wonderful news!" said Ivy. "I have a bottle of champagne around here somewhere. Let me get it." She disappeared through the parlor to the kitchen, Merritt trailing behind her.

"He took that well," he whispered to Claudia.

She beamed up at him. "I knew he would. He's not an ogre."

"Do you suppose they exist, too?"

"Possibly." She leaned against him. "Can we do a toast? I've never done one before."

He pressed a kiss to the top of her head. "We'll toast to whatever we want."

ABOUT THE AUTHOR

Jessica Marting is a sci-fi and paranormal romance author, art enthusiast (not quite an artist, despite all that time in art school), an avid reader, and makeup collector. She lives in Toronto.

For updates about books, giveaways, and other fun stuff, subscribe to her newsletter: jessicamarting.com/newsletter

The Commons

Supernova

Celestial Chaos

Standalone Novels & Novellas

Spindle's End

Trade Secrets

Neon Vice

Dead Ringer

Escape From Europa 10

Castaways

Demon's Favor

Her Purrfect Match

Rapture